HUSKY VALLEY

COMPLETE SERIES

LEXI HAYES

Published by No Regerts Press, LLC

NO REGERTS
PRESS, LLC

Cover Designed by Cormar Covers

ISBN 978-1-957933-21-4 (print)

Join my mailing list here:
www.lexihayes.com

CONTENTS

CUFFED BY THE SHERIFF

TEASED BY THE MAILMAN

CATFISHED BY THE IT GUY

PLOWED BY THE FARMER

CUFFED BY THE SHERIFF

CHAPTER 1
JUNIPER

The entire world outside is a swirling mass of white as I grip the steering wheel like it's a lifeline.

"Come on, come *on*," I mutter, leaning forward in the vain hope that being closer to the windshield will help me see better. The road is nearly invisible, just a vague, icy path ahead, flanked by towering snowbanks that threaten to close in on me further with each passing minute.

I start to skid, and my heart leaps into my throat. I ease off the gas, hoping that will help, but the car feels like it has a mind of its own, every slight bump in the road sending it sliding out of control.

Why didn't I listen when Kyle told me to get new tires?

The car weaves back and forth as the rear wheels skate to the left, then to the right.

Every muscle in my body is coiled tight as I try to keep the car straight. The tires skid on the icy road again, even worse this time. "Crap!" I yelp, correcting the wheel with a quick turn. The car responds, but barely. I can feel my panic rising.

"Juniper, chill out," I whisper to myself, my voice shaky. "Slow and steady, no sudden moves. Just relax—"

As if on cue, the car hits a patch of ice, and suddenly, everything goes wrong. The back end fishtails wildly, and the tires completely lose their grip on the road. The car starts to spin in a circle, and I scream, instinctively yanking the wheel in a desperate attempt to straighten it out. "For god's sake!!!"

It's no use. I stomp on the brakes, but it only makes things worse, my trusty sedan skidding with a gracelessness that's both horrifying and impressive, ending up nose-first in a ditch.

For a moment, I just sit there willing my breathing to return to normal, my hands still clutching the steering wheel and my heart pounding so hard I can hear it throughout the car. Everything else has gone eerily still, like I've been swallowed up by the storm.

"Fantastic," I groan, staring at the fluffy white barrier that's swallowed up my bumper.

I check my phone—dead, of course. Rifling through the chaos of my duffle bag, fingers searching through the tangle of earphones and chocolate bar wrappers, I finally find the external battery.

It's ice-cold and a long shot, but it's all I have. I plug in the phone and wait for it to charge enough to turn on.

The car heater hums, battling the creeping cold valiantly as I sit wrapped in my lucky (ha!) sweater, which is cozy, but woefully inadequate for this weather. I tuck my legs under me and watch the snowflakes dance dizzily outside. Each twirling flake seems to mock my questionable life choices.

"Why does everything have to be so hard?" I groan, resisting the urge to cry.

Worst. Day. Ever.

It had started with my hasty exit from a job that was going nowhere, the final straw being a boss who thought "no" was just a suggestion and who had uttered a screeched threat to have me arrested after kneeing him in the junk. The cherry on top had been my parents' advice to apologize to the asshole to try and get my job back. And now this!

"Fuck no!" I yell, half expecting my car to offer some moral support. Kyle would know what to say if he were here. I could always count on my brother to have my back. The lucky guy had managed to escape our parents' clutches and rebuilt his life in Deepwood Mountain, working as a motorcycle mechanic for McCafferty Customs.

My snap decision to quit was supposed to be my turn to get a fresh start. If only I could get out of this snowy trap! I peer hopefully at my phone. Still not charged enough to power on.

I turn up the radio and an old country tune begins. Soon I'm belting out the lyrics with more enthusiasm than skill. My Chucks are propped up on the dashboard, my makeshift concert hall blissfully private until a sharp rap on the window has me jumping out of my skin and twisting toward the sound.

Standing right outside is a massive male figure, clad in a thick dark brown jacket with a black felt cowboy hat, and a star-shaped badge that glints menacingly at me through the snowstorm.

Shit—it's a cop.

"You okay, Ma'am?" he begins, pressing closer to the window. "Need a tow?"

I turn down the radio hastily. *What am I going to do? What if that sleazeball Gary did in fact file a police report? I don't want to go to jail. Not when I'm so close to Kyle's place.*

I crack the window open, eyeing him warily. "May I please see your ID?" I ask, my voice steadier than I feel.

He taps the shiny badge on the left side of his jacket. "Right here, Ma'am." Then he points to his name on the right. "Sheriff Quinn," he says, tipping his hat.

"How do I know that badge isn't a fake? Let me see it up close."

With a sigh that suggests I'm testing his nerves, he squats down to my eye level as I roll down the window a little more. Up close, he seems even larger, his presence almost over-whelming. But he smells like pine—and something else, sweet and comforting. He glances at me with gorgeous brown eyes, and I register his full beard dotted with gray, and his sensual mouth—

Focus, Juniper.

He leans closer, letting me inspect the badge. I reach out to touch it, wishing I was touching his broad chest. His breath is so warm, in contrast to the biting air around us.

"Satisfied?" His voice has turned into a deep rumble, and it sends an unbidden shiver down my spine.

I shake my head. "You have any other identification? You might be one of those psychos who impersonates cops to...well, *you know*..."

He scoffs. "You think I wear this uniform for fun?"

Well, I'm *having fun watching you wear it—*

JUNIPER!!!

I can't help myself as I let my gaze drift over the rest of him. "I don't know," I shrug. "Looks a little tight on you. Straining in some places, even. How do I know you're really Sheriff Quinn?"

With a huff, he stands, stepping back from the car. "I'll get my ID card," he grumbles. "*And* the equipment to pull your car out. You're welcome."

I watch him retreat, my mind racing. *Damn him!* Why does he have to be so attractive? Thick in all the right places. Those soulful eyes. Kissable lips...

What's the matter with me? I need to get out of here before he runs my name. I glance toward the road, remembering a cabin not far back. Maybe, just maybe I could make it there and avoid any more complications. I don't need a sheriff calling my parents—or worse, stumbling across a police report from my former boss.

As he walks away, I steel myself. The moment he's far enough away, I'll make a run for that cabin. Fresh starts don't come along that often, and I'm not about to let a sexy sheriff in a *very* well-fitting uniform slow me down.

CHAPTER 2
ISAAC

The snow might be muffling the world around me, but inside, everything is suddenly too loud. I've grown accustomed to the silence that's settled in ever since my wife Deb passed away seven years ago. Cancer's a bitch. It took her and left me merely going through the motions of life, my heart numb, my days blending together into one long, cold winter.

But the young woman in the ditch today, with eyes as blue as the heart of an iceberg, has left me reeling and jolted me back to life—an electric spark, unexpected and... *unsettling*. I've never had such an intense reaction to someone before.

I'm being ridiculous. A pretty little thing like her wouldn't spare a second glance at a washed-up old sheriff who's more donut than deputy these days. Her comment about my tight uniform said it all—she probably thought this pathetic old man needed not only to get a life, but also to lay off the carbs.

I fumble in the back of my SUV, grabbing my ID card and the tow strap. As I glance back, her car door swings open and I see her dart through the thickening snow.

What in the—

Instinct and my training kick in, and I'm chasing her on

foot before I know it. The cold bites at my face as I barrel forward into the blizzard, snow whipping around me in furious swirls. She's got a few yards' lead on me, her figure barely visible through the whiteout, but I can still make out her determined stride as she plows through the drifts.

"Stop!" I shout, my voice struggling to compete with the howling wind. But she doesn't. She doesn't even glance back as she pushes forward, trying to outrun me. The snow is deep, and she sinks down a little more with each step. I worry that her clothes offer little protection against this god-awful weather and the drifts that threaten to swallow her up. Why isn't she wearing a coat?

My heart pounds in my chest, my breath coming out in harsh puffs. She's slowing now, stumbling, her sneakers slipping on the frozen patches of ice hidden beneath the snow. I watch as she fights to keep her balance. It's clear she's running on pure adrenaline at this point, driven by a mix of fear, frustration, and maybe even a touch of defiance. But that will only take her so far.

"Damn it, you're going to get yourself killed!" I growl as I give chase, my frustration mounting.

Just as I'm about to reach her, she stumbles as she takes a sharp turn, veering toward a clump of trees. It slows her down and gives me the opening I need. I push harder. The wind whips around us, icy and unforgiving, but I barely notice it. All I can think about is getting to her before she hurts herself.

She makes it to the edge of the tree line, her breath coming in ragged gasps. For a moment she hesitates, nervously glancing back over her shoulder, and that's when I make my move. With a final burst of speed, I leap forward, reaching out to grab her.

She yelps in surprise as I catch hold of her, our

momentum sending us down together, the snow cushioning our fall. She kicks and flails underneath me, but I tighten my grip on her.

"Let me go!" she cries.

"Not a chance," I grunt, holding her close as she tries to wiggle out from under me. "You're not running off into a blizzard, Ma'am, not on my watch."

She fights for another few moments, but I'm too strong, too big, and too determined. Slowly, her struggles begin to fade, exhaustion and the cold sapping her energy and the fight draining out of her when she realizes she's not going to win this one.

"You done?" I ask, my voice softer now.

She lets out a frustrated sigh, finally giving in. "I wasn't... I wasn't trying to cause trouble," she mumbles, her breath hitching.

"I know," I say, loosening my grip just enough to roll back and get up, pulling her up with me. "But it's not smart to run off in the middle of a snowstorm."

She huffs. "I didn't ask for your advice, Sheriff."

"I realize that," I agree, guiding her back toward the car, the wind whipping in our faces. "You're getting it anyway."

As we trudge back through the snow, I keep a firm hold on her, half-expecting her to try to make another run for it. But she seems to have resigned herself to the situation, and her steps are slow and reluctant as we approach my SUV.

"Hands behind your back," I instruct.

"Wait...what are you—"

I get out my handcuffs. "I'm sorry, Ma'am. You're a flight risk."

She rolls her eyes as I secure the cuffs on her wrists.

"You going to frisk me, too? I mean, I might have a stash of candy bars in my bra."

I snort. "Is that another crack about my weight? Or a bribe?"

"*Another* crack?" She furrows her brow. "What was the first?"

"Never mind. Look, I won't frisk you if you tell me what your name is."

She sighs, then blows a blonde curl out her face. "Juniper. Juniper Shaw."

"Where's your driver's license, Ms. Shaw?" I ask, her name pinging my memory, making me wonder if she is related to Kyle Shaw in town.

She doesn't answer.

"You do *have* a driver's license, right?"

"Yes!" she finally exclaims. "It's just...oh, what does it matter," she grumbles under her breath, huffing and tilting her head to the side. "Hidden pocket in my yoga pants. Right thigh."

I reach down and slide my thumb over the outside of her thigh. Thankfully, I feel the edge of the plastic right away. I slip my fingers into the pocket, pull out the card, and almost choke when I glance at it.

21?! So young. Way too young for me to be having these confusing thoughts about her. And also *way* too young to be mixed up in...well, whatever mess she's clearly got going on.

"Let's get you out of the cold before you freeze to death," I say, opening the back door of the SUV and helping her in.

Once I get in the front and crank the heat, I turn to her in the back. "I get that you're scared, but you don't need to be. You're safe now, okay?"

She looks up at me, her expression guarded, but there's a flicker of something else in her bright blue eyes—reluctant trust, maybe. Even interest?

Yeah, keep dreamin', old man.

"Call me Juniper," she whispers.

"Why did you run, Juniper?" I ask softly.

She shakes her head, gazing blankly out the window. I wait as patiently as I can, letting my eyes take in the wavy blonde hair that falls to her chin, the button nose, and the delicate column of her neck. She sighs and worries at her lush little bottom lip. Finally, her story pours out—her job at the bar, her sleazy boss, her fear of him pressing charges for kneeing him in the balls after he groped her, and lastly her parents' reaction to it all.

My blood boils.

Why are people so fucking shitty? It makes me want to pound the dashboard. "I can arrest that bastard for assault, if you want," I mutter, my words coming out more of a growl than I intended. "Men like that deserve to face consequences." I stare ahead, picturing giving the asshole a fitting punishment courtesy my steel-toed boots.

When I finally come out of that daydream, she's watching me and shifting uncomfortably in the seat. "You really think the police would take my side?" she asks doubtfully, her tone hinting at years of disappointment.

"If I'm the one handling it? One hundred percent." My response is firm, intended to reassure her. "I don't have any time for bullies or cowards. Neither does the law."

She avoids my eyes. "I'm sorry. I wasn't thinking straight when I decided to run. You had me all…flustered."

Flustered? As in…? Nah. She just means anxious because I'm a cop. The police have that effect on a lot of people. Especially ones that've had trouble with the authorities before.

When I turn to the computer on the dash, she noticeably stiffens in the back seat.

"You okay?" I ask.

"Just fine," she chirps.

Hmm. When I run her ID, I see a list of minor offenses. Nothing terrible, but enough to paint a picture of a young life on the edge and for her to be worried about. "Sounds like you've had it rough," I say. A wave a fury ripples through me as I consider that someone had left this poor young woman thinking that crime was a viable option.

"Life didn't so much *give* me lemons as hurl them at me." She shrugs, a wry smile playing on her sexy lips.

"I guess you learned to dodge pretty fast, then," I reply, giving her a small, empathetic grin.

"I prefer to think I hurled them back."

I'm laughing at that when my radio crackles to life. "Sheriff, we've got a full-blown blizzard coming in fast." Hallie's voice from Dispatch is urgent.

A blizzard—not surprising, given what we've dealt with so far. I look at Juniper, this unexpected storm of a girl who's somehow stirred something in me. "Looks like we're stuck with each other for a bit," I say. "Honestly, I hope you *do* have some candy bars in your bra, because we're gonna need 'em."

CHAPTER 3
JUNIPER

Sitting in the back of Sheriff Quinn's SUV, I can't seem to stop thinking about him. I know I should be frightened... of the relentless snow, of a small-town sheriff I've never met, of the whole situation. But instead, I find myself oddly comforted by the thought of spending more time with the man. Comforted and, unbelievably... *aroused.*

What the hell?

I didn't expect a chase through the snow to be so erotic. But...*yeah.* When he caught me, his weight pinning me down, his breath heavy and hot in my ear, growling my name, I didn't want it to end.

I legit nearly told him I was hiding a weapon on me, just so he'd frisk me...*thoroughly.* The thought of his hands all over my body makes my insides squirm and my panties seriously wet.

There's something about him that I'm a complete sucker for: not just his rugged good looks and extra thick body, but the way he moves with purpose, the way his voice carries both authority and warmth, like he's spent a lifetime protecting people and he's *damn good* at it. I've seen his kind before—the proverbial strong, silent type—but there's a softness to him too, an empathetic look in his brown eyes that makes me wonder what's going on behind them.

The way he handled everything tonight—so calm, so in control—should have annoyed me. I'm not used to people taking charge of my life, least of all a man who looks like he stepped right out of "big and tall" catalog. But I'm intrigued. I want to know more.

Where's he from? What's he into? What's he like when he's not wearing that tight uniform and playing the part of town protector?

And, the million-dollar question, what does he think about *me?*

Am I just another damsel in distress in his eyes? Yet one more girl who's made a mess of her life and needs rescuing? Or does he sense that there's more to me than that? The way his dark eyes study me—like he's seeing past all my attitude and sarcasm—I think *maybe* he does.

I catch a glimpse of him in the rearview mirror, his face illuminated by the soft glow of the dashboard lights as he speaks with Dispatch. His voice is a low, steady rumble, but there's a tension there too, a pulsing in his temple that tells me he's not exactly thrilled about our current situation. Is that just about the storm? Could it possibly be about me?

Shit. I really need to get a hold of myself.

"Hallie, there's a cabin nearby—vacation rental, currently unoccupied. Requesting permission to hole up there until the storm clears." Sheriff Quinn's words slice through my thoughts.

There's a pause, filled with the hum of the SUV's heater and my own anxious breathing. Then Dispatch crackles back. "Permission granted, Sheriff. Stay put till the blizzard passes. Keep your radio on for updates."

Sheriff Quinn turns to me. "Are there things in your car you need?"

"It's all in my duffle bag in the passenger seat."

Before I can blink, he's stepping out into the whirling snow. The cold blasts in the moment the door opens, reminding me just how inadequate my attire is. He trudges to my car, his figure outlined against the swirling white, and returns shortly with my bag slung over his shoulder and—surprisingly—a few candy bars clutched in his hand.

"I found the real hiding place," he winks, a smile playing at the corners of his mouth as he sticks them in his jacket pocket. He stands in front of my door, blocking the snow and wind. "You promise not to run off again if I take off the cuffs?"

"Cross my heart." I smile and give him a nod.

I exhale deeply as he unlocks them. The relief of being uncuffed is immense. I rub my wrists, which are a little tender. "Thank you, Sheriff."

"You're welcome," he says. "And just Isaac is fine, by the way." He shuts my door and goes around to get into the driver's seat.

Isaac. I like it.

The drive is slow, the SUV's headlights barely cutting through the thick curtain of snow, the world outside reduced to a blur of white and the occasional shadowy outline of trees. When we arrive, we dash together from the SUV to the shelter of the cabin, Isaac right next to me with our bags, the cold nipping at our heels.

The cabin is a standard two-room setup: kitchen and living room in one area, bedroom and bathroom in the other. It's not an upscale rental by any stretch, but it's clean and neat with working appliances, a sofa and recliner, and a four-person dining table. Everything is done in wood—walls, floor, furniture.

Isaac wastes no time once we're inside. He moves around the space with a practiced ease that suggests he's done this a hundred times. Within minutes, he has a fire crackling merrily in the fireplace, its glow battling the chill still clinging to my bones. The welcome aroma of coffee soon fills the air as he sets it to brew, mingling with the scent of pine from all the wood. It's comforting and homey.

As Isaac grabs a big pot from a rack above the counter, he glances over and notices me desperately trying not to shiver, to no avail. "Go change into something dry and warm. If you don't have anything in that bag of yours that will work, there should be something in the bedroom."

I'm too cold to do much else but mock salute and follow his instructions.

The bedroom is small but has a big bed covered in pillows and soft blankets. I briefly contemplate stripping and rolling around in them, waiting for Isaac to come find me—

What is with me? I'm losing it.

The chest of drawers is full of warm clothes. I guess a lot of people who rent this place don't bring appropriate clothing for the Deepwood Mountain weather. I pull on some flannel pajamas that are a few sizes too big but blessedly warm. They smell faintly of cedar and mothballs, a scent that instantly makes me think of my grandmother's house and is strangely comforting, triggering memories of happier times before my parents drank themselves into oblivion.

Once dressed, I use my now-charged phone to call Kyle.

"Juniper! You okay?" he asks, his tone his typical big brother mix of concern and irritation.

"I'm fine. Got stuck in the snowstorm, but I'm safe at a cabin," I assure him.

There's a pause, then Kyle sighs. "A cabin? Where? Are you alone?" His voice is exasperated. "Seriously, Junie, this is no time to be vague. I know you're a magnet for chaos, but..."

"What can I say? It's a talent. You know, like your ability to fix a motor bike with two inches of duct tape and a stapler."

He snorts. "*My* talents don't usually involve braving life-threatening weather."

"Hey, it's okay. I'm with Sheriff...Quinn, I think?...in a rental cabin in the mountains."

"The sheriff?" He groans. "Oh god. What did you do this time?"

"I'm *fine*."

There's a long pause. I can totally picture the expression on his face. "You're in handcuffs right now, aren't you." Damn, he knows me well.

I laugh. "Not anymore, I'm not." I clear my throat. "I'll see you tomorrow, Kyle. Bye!"

I end the call and stuff my phone in my pocket. My phone buzzes with a bunch of text notifications that I missed, but I'll reply later. I chuckle, feeling a pang of longing for the banter and comfort only my brother can provide. Can he handle me being back in his life full-time again? I hope so.

Returning to the combined kitchen and living area, I find Isaac ladling soup into two bowls. He looks up, a hint of a smile on his face. "Soup's ready. Hope you like chicken noodle. It was either that or a mystery can with no label that might be older than both of us together."

"Chicken noodle sounds great, thanks," I reply, sitting at the small dining table. The warmth from the fire wraps around us, a stark contrast to the howl of the wind outside. While I was on the phone Isaac must've changed his clothes. He's removed his uniform shirt and replaced it with a light blue flannel over his white undershirt. On the bottom he's now wearing a pair of dark blue sweatpants with *sheriff* running down the side of one leg and worn sneakers.

He looks like sex on a stick.

Ahem. "Those mystery cans are I think best reserved for extreme emergencies, like the end of the world…or college finals."

He chuckles, his smiling eyes reflecting the firelight, and we dig in. The rich, savory broth instantly chases away the last of the chill in my bones.

"So…last name Shaw…is Kyle Shaw your brother, by any chance?" Isaac asks. "Haven't seen him in a while. How's he doing?"

I blink, surprised that he knows my brother. But then again, it's a small town. "Yep, Kyle's my older brother. He's great. Busy, as always. But loving his job at McCafferty Customs."

He nods. "Glad to hear it. Dash and his buddies there are good people." He licks his spoon with that big tongue and time goes sideways for me for a beat. I clench my thighs.

My *god.*

Focus, Juniper. He's talking about your brother. We don't need to be stirring those two thoughts together right now. Gross.

"I remember Kyle mentioning you a few times," he continues, and I mentally slap myself back to the conversation. "Said you were tough. He seemed proud of you."

I shake off my ill-timed arousal. "Aww, that's sweet. He's always been the responsible one, the one who had to grow up too fast."

I stir my soup, thinking about what he had to go through. He wanted me to get out and come with him, but at the time I thought I could help my parents. If only I could get them to stay in rehab, they'd be okay, you know? Kyle had told me it was a lost cause, that they had to want to help themselves. I guess I eventually learned that the hard way.

"It's weird," I continue. "Even when he's not around, I can hear his voice in the back of my mind, telling me not to do anything stupid." I let out a long sigh. "Didn't work so well tonight."

Isaac leans back in his chair, stroking his beard. Wow, his hands are big, too. "Considering the circumstances," he says slowly, "I'd say you've done pretty well so far."

"Thanks…I think." I grin. "But you haven't known me long enough to see my worst decisions. Kyle's usually the one who bails me out."

"Sounds like he's been a good brother," he remarks.

"He really has," I agree, my tone softening. "He's the best."

"You're lucky. I don't have any brothers or sisters." His smile is wistful. "Sometimes I wish I did."

"Seriously. I don't know what I would do without my brother. He taught me everything I know."

I finish up the last of my soup. "Delicious. I bet you were a boy scout, Isaac. You're way too good at all this stuff—starting a fire, cooking. What other talents do you have?"

His cheeks flush red as he suddenly busies himself with cleaning up the dishes. "I only opened a can…but yeah, I was an Eagle Scout, actually," he murmurs.

"I'm not at all surprised," I chuckle. "Let me help."

"No," he says, firmly, and blocks me from the counter with his bulky arm. "Go warm yourself by the fire."

I huff playfully. "Fine." I retreat to the couch, draping my legs over the arm of it. I stretch my bare feet out toward the flames, trying to bring them back to life, but they're still numb from the cold.

"My feet feel like two ice blocks," I grumble.

Isaac turns off the water and walks over to me. He sits in the recliner across from me and pats his lap invitingly. "Put 'em here."

I obey, sliding my feet over his fleece-covered thighs. Oh dear… This could be disastrous.

He takes my feet in his hands, and I stifle a whimper. I guess they do have some feeling in them: he's killing me right now as his warm fingers rub patterns over my skin, sending sparks to every nerve ending. The man is definitely getting my circulation going—*everywhere*. His touch is firm, but still somehow achingly gentle in his exploration of my skin, the roughness of his palms a sharp contrast to the tenderness of his actions.

He gives equal attention to my heels, my arches, the balls of my feet, even each toe, his large hands surprisingly deft. I'm melting into the cushions of the couch, hoping I don't suddenly do something embarrassing like let out a loud moan.

"That's really nice," I say on a soft sigh, my head falling back.

No one has ever taken care of me like this, not with such genuine concern. I've never experienced this kind of treatment from any man, let alone a cop.

He looks up, meeting my gaze. "Can't have these cute little toes frozen, now can we?" His voice is deep and just a bit hoarse, and it gets me going all over again.

I feel my cheeks heat—and not just from the fire. There's something so steady, safe and, weirdly, *soft* about him, despite his big, gruff, and intimidating appearance. I've always been wary of those in authority, but with Isaac, it's different. Even in this strange, tense situation, I feel safe. It's a feeling I haven't had in a long time…maybe never.

We sit there in silence, the crackling fire the only sound as he continues to massage my feet. I lean back, allowing myself to relax for the first time in what feels like forever. This moment, however fleeting, is something I never expected to find—a brief, precious reprieve from the chaos of my messy life.

CHAPTER 4
ISAAC

What the hell am I thinking, giving this little spitfire a foot massage? Who *am* I?

I mean, dammit, I never even gave *Deb* a foot massage.

I hadn't realized how much I'd missed simple human contact. The feel of this girl's skin, the way she's relaxing under my touch—it's awakened something in me that I've tried to ignore for years.

I want more of it. More of her.

Those feelings are terrifying. I'm not sure I'm ready to open that door again, to make myself vulnerable to another human being.

But for whatever reason, Juniper makes me want to.

She's a burst of sunlight on a cloudy, stormy day—invigorating, unexpected, and stirring up feelings inside me that I thought would never stretch awake again after Deb. It's been so long since I've felt this...*alive*. She's young, vibrant, and despite the tough life she's led, there's a spark in her that draws me in.

It's more than just her resilience; it's her humor, her sass, the way she doesn't back down even when frankly she probably should.

It all only makes me want to take care of her. Protect her. Take her away from those rotten parents. And *definitely* give that asshole boss a beating he'll never forget.

Now, rubbing her soft feet, I'm fantasizing about slipping her sweet little toes into my mouth. That would be my preferred way to warm up any part of her, actually. But that's just the secret fantasy of a dirty old man.

When she finally lifts her head, she gazes at me lazily with those heavenly blue eyes, and I melt.

"What's your story?" she asks, her voice a little husky. I'm hoping I'm doing that with my touch, but I'm not going to hold my breath.

"I've been the sheriff here for the past ten years. Grew up in this town, so it just kinda made sense to stick around and keep the place safe. Before that, I was just a regular guy, doing regular things. Joined the force right after high school, worked my way up." I hold her feet that have settled comfortably in my lap.

She leans on the couch arm and smiles. "So, you're like a hometown hero, huh? Bet you know everyone and everything that goes on around here."

"Pretty much," I admit, feeling a bit self-conscious under her scrutiny. "Not much happens here that doesn't get around, that's for sure."

She nods thoughtfully, then asks the question that makes my stomach tighten. "Are you married?"

For a moment, I hesitate. "I was," I finally say quietly.

"Divorced?" she probes gently.

I shake my head, my gaze dropping to the floor. "Widowed. She died of cancer a few years back."

Juniper's expression softens. "Fuck, I'm sorry," she

murmurs, then, after a beat, adds, "You wanna tell me about her?"

I look at her, startled by the request. It's not something people usually ask, not in a way that makes you feel like they truly want to know. But there's something in this girl's beautiful eyes, a kindness and a willingness to listen, that makes me want to open up.

I take a deep breath, staring into the flames. "Deb was... She was the kind of person who made you feel lucky to just know her. She had a way of brightening any room right when she stepped into it. We met in high school. I was the awkward, tall kid in the back of the class, and she was the girl everyone wanted to be friends with. The only way I could catch her eye was to do something really crazy."

Juniper grins widely, clearly intrigued. "Oh yeah? What did you do?"

I smile at the memory. "I knew she liked daisies, so I went to the flower shop and bought enough to fill her whole locker. When she opened it, daisies spilled out everywhere. I should've just given them to her like a normal person. But instead, I ended up having to stay after school to clean everything up. She stayed to help me."

She giggles, the sound light and genuine. "That's incredibly sweet...and a *little* over-the-top."

"Yeah, well, subtlety was never my strong suit," I admit. "She loved it, though. Said it was the most romantic thing anyone had ever done for her. From then on, that was it. We were inseparable. She wasn't just my girlfriend, but my best friend too."

I pause, the smile fading as the memories turn somber. "We got married young, not long after graduation. She worked as a secretary for St. Gabriel's, the Catholic church in town. We never had kids. I always thought we had plenty of time for that, but now…" I shrug. "I regret not starting a family earlier."

Juniper doesn't speak, just sips her coffee quietly. I expect to see pity in her eyes, but instead, I find a comforting understanding.

I lean back in my chair. "What about you? Married? Boyfriend? Someone who's going to come looking for you if you don't check in, besides your brother?" If she says she has a romantic partner, I don't know what I'll do.

She shakes her head, and shrugs. "Nope. No husband, no boyfriend, not even a pet rock. My life is pretty much work, work, and more work."

I raise an eyebrow curiously, admiring the way the firelight dances in her eyes. "And besides the scumbag of a boss, how was that?"

She snorts, rolling her eyes. "It was a good week if I managed to change the beer kegs without dropping one on my foot. Believe me, I did that more times than I'd like to admit."

"Sounds painful." I don't want to imagine these pretty little feet on my lap getting crunched by kegs.

"And of course there were all the drunks who'd cuss me out if I took too long with their order, hit on me, and throw things at me to get my attention."

"Unacceptable," I grunt angrily through gritted teeth.

"As for dating…" She sighs. "I didn't have time. I was working as many hours as I could at the bar, trying to make enough money to support my parents and myself. They drank away every penny I gave them. I thought I could change them by being a responsible, dutiful daughter…" She sighs again. "Nope."

I frown. "I'm really sorry you had to deal with all that. It sounds like a lot. I'm glad you at least had your brother for support."

She nods, a fond smile briefly lighting up her face. "Kyle always told me I could come stay with him if it got too much. Said he'd kick my ass for working myself to the bone for those two." She pauses, a hint of sadness creeping into her voice. "I never wanted to rely on him, you know? But now... I think I really need to. So I hope he meant it."

I lean forward, sliding my hand over her ankle. My thumb unconsciously drifts back and forth over her soft skin, and the simple contact sends an electric jolt through me. "Sometimes, asking for help is the hardest thing to do. But I don't think it makes you weak. If anything, it shows you're strong enough to admit you can't do it all on your own."

She looks at me, and for a second, I lose myself in the depths of her eyes. The air seems thick with a charged tension. Her lips part slightly, and it takes everything I have to resist the sudden, inexplicable urge to pull her to me and kiss her.

Then she swallows, dropping her eyes, and the moment passes. "I guess I just didn't want to be another burden," she whispers.

I shake my head, smiling softly and patting her ankle. "From what I've seen, you're anything but a burden. Besides," I smirk, trying to lighten the mood, "Kyle's probably been dying for a chance to boss you around again."

She laughs, and the sound swirls low in my belly. "It's downright weird how well you know him."

CHAPTER 5
JUNIPER

Laughing with Isaac feels as natural as breathing. Every moment I spend with him, I find myself more comfortable, like we've known each other for years. Our playful banter slips under my skin and lingers there, giving me butterflies that flutter low…deliciously low…in my belly.

"So, Isaac," I say, setting down my coffee mug. "What do you like to do for fun when you're not busy sheriff-ing?"

He looks at me, a wistful smile on his lips. "I, uh, haven't had much of that lately. Mostly, I just work."

An ache throbs deep in my heart. "What did you and Deb like to do together?"

He hesitates. Then sighs, as if deciding to let me in just a little more. "We used to go dancing."

"Really?" I ask, unable to hide my excitement. "What kind of dancing?"

"Country, at the Rustic Ridge Bar," he replies. "Line dancing, the Two-Step, you name it."

"Now you're talking, Sheriff. I love music and dancing. I'll be right back." I grin and run into the bedroom, returning with my phone. I quickly find a country playlist and set my phone on the table. The first upbeat song fills the room and I start swaying to the rhythm. "Come on, big guy! Show me what you've got."

He shakes his head, scratching his jaw. "I don't think so."

"What, are you afraid you're past your prime? Or are you too chicken to show me your moves?"

Isaac rolls his eyes, but I swear there's a spark in them all of a sudden. "You think I can't keep up, kid?"

I laugh, twirling around. "Prove me wrong, *Pops*."

He arches his brow, and then with a resigned but amused sigh, Isaac gets up. He crosses to me in a few quick strides, reaches out and grabs my hand, spinning me around before pulling me in to start a *very* close two-step. The sudden press of his strong, solid body against mine catches me off guard. He fits against me seamlessly, even with our size difference. It's like dancing with a graceful bear.

We glide across the living room, our movements in perfect sync. It feels instinctive, like we've been doing this together for ages. He doesn't step on my feet once! I can't stop smiling, and the laughter bubbles up out of us as we playfully navigate the limited space. Isaac dips me, and I let out a startled giggle, the world tilting before he pulls me back up again.

The next song is slower, and he holds me even closer. I can feel every part of his body against mine...especially the hard length nestled against my belly. His sweatpants do nothing to hide that beast.

And I don't mind at all.

My heart races as I look up at him. There's a heat in his gaze that sends a shiver down my spine. One of his hands is resting gently on my back and the other is holding my own, guiding me through the slow, intimate dance.

The world around us fades away as I rest my cheek on his chest, wanting to rub against him like a kitten. It's just the two of us, swaying together to the music. His hand moves up to my neck, threading his fingers through my hair. It sends electric sparks shooting through my entire body, and heat pooling in my core. I tilt my head back into his hand and feel his breath on my face, warm and inviting. He searches my eyes, silently asking for permission.

"Kiss me," I whisper, aching for his touch. "Please, Isaac."

He groans, his voice deep and gravelly, as if I squeezed the air right out of him with my words. He begins to lean down, then suddenly pulls back, his eyes filled with regret. "I'm sorry, Juniper," he murmurs.

I stare at him, stunned, my heart still pounding.

"I shouldn't…" He looks away, running a hand through his hair. "I just… I don't want to complicate things."

A flush of embarrassment floods my cheeks, and I can feel them turning a bright, fiery red.

Oh god, how could I have read that all wrong?

"N-no, it's my fault," I stammer, desperately trying to keep the tears at bay. I untangle myself from his arms. "I need some air. Excuse me." I bolt for the back door before he can say anything, the cold blast of the blizzard hitting me like a wall the moment I step outside.

"Juniper, wait!" Isaac calls. But I've already taken off. The snow swirling around me in a dizzying blur and the icy wind nipping at my skin are nothing compared to the searing mortification burning through me. My bare feet sink deeper into the snow with every step, the cold slicing like tiny blades, but I welcome the pain—it's something to focus on instead of my embarrassment.

I push myself harder, my legs battling through the thick drifts as if I can outrun the crushing shame, confusion, and stupid longing that got me into this mess. Behind me, Isaac's heavy footsteps grow louder, the crunch of snow under his shoes heavy and relentless, like he's hunting me down.

"Juniper!" he yells again, his voice carrying a mix of anger, concern, and something else—something wild and passionate that makes my core catch fire.

What? What is going on? How does this man do this to me?

I can't face him. Not after I basically begged him to kiss me, like a silly lovesick girl, only to have him reject me—worse, *almost* kiss me and then stop! I run faster, my breath coming out in frantic, uneven puffs, my lungs burning. My mind is a chaotic storm raging as hard as the one around us, my thoughts crashing into each other with bewildering speed.

I should've known better. But there was something in his eyes, in his touch... Something that grabbed hold of my heart and made me think he wanted me as much as I wanted him. I guess I thought wrong.

"Goddammit, Juniper!" Isaac's voice is closer now, laced with raw emotion that sends an unholy shiver down my spine, wrenching each nerve as it goes. There's a primal edge to his growl, something that makes me run even faster, as if doing so could force him to make that sound again. Deep down, I know I can't outrun him. He's too strong, too determined. The thought excites me in a way I don't understand.

My foot catches on a hidden root and I stumble, my body pitching forward. The snow cushions my fall, but it's a harsh, icy embrace. I scramble to get up, but before I can, Isaac's thick body is pinning me to the ground—heavy, warm, and unyielding.

"Get off me. Let me go!" I gasp, fighting against him, my pulse hammering in my ears. I don't really want him to do any such thing. I *love* the feel of his massive body on top of me, his breath hot against my ear, his voice a low, rough plea. "Please,

Juniper, stop struggling. You don't know what this does to me."

Is he as turned on as I am? Are we both a little crazy?

My emotions are a wild, tangled mess. I don't know whether I want to scream, cry, *or come.*

As I writhe under him, I can feel his hard cock pressing against my ass.

Fuck.

"Juniper, you keep this up much longer and I'll be coming in my pants," he groans, sounding more desperate with every ragged breath. His hand thrusts into my hair, and his grip tightens, sharp tingles exploding all over my scalp.

"God, that's so hot!" I exclaim, and he unleashes a gritty moan as his teeth sink into the nape of my neck, near the hairline.

I cry out, nearly climaxing then and there when I feel his hot tongue glide over my flesh.

"I love the chase, the capture..." He pauses to run his lips over the shell of my ear and I tremble. "*Devouring* my sweet prey."

I whimper at his words, my arousal skyrocketing.

"I... I thought you didn't want me," I begin.

He nuzzles my neck. "*I shouldn't* doesn't mean *I don't want to*...and trust me, I do."

"Why shouldn't you?" I ask, closing my eyes.

He sighs. "Because you're so young, so sweet, so full of life." He rolls off me, getting onto his knees. "I'm just a sad old man who should know better. I'm—"

"Ridiculously undervaluing yourself," I say, before using my momentary freedom to jump up and run.

"Why you little—!" he yells in a combination of mock anger and amusement. It sends a thrill through me, half-excitement, half-fear, knowing he's not far behind me. I can hear his footsteps crunching through the snow, getting louder, closer, each one promising that he's going to catch me.

Up ahead, I spot the dark outline of a small shed against the white landscape. I make a desperate dash for it, my breath coming in short, sharp gasps. The snowdrifts are deeper here, dragging my legs down, but I push through.

Just as I reach the shed, my fingers fumbling at the handle, the ground trembles beneath me as Isaac bears down on me. I barely manage to yank the door open before his body collides with mine, knocking the breath from my lungs. His thick arms wrap around me, pulling me back against his solid chest, capturing me in a firm grip.

A surprised laugh escapes me, mingled with the rapid thud of my heart. "Let me go, you big brute!" I gasp, but my words lack any real conviction. There's a buzz in the chase, a playful fire between us that crackles with energy, and being caught is as exhilarating for me as the hunt itself.

"Not a chance," he growls, making me tremble. He effortlessly lifts me off the ground. My feet dangle for a moment, kicking at the air as he holds me to him, his broad chest solid and warm against my back.

Isaac kicks the shed door open sending it slamming against the wall with a resounding thud. He rushes us inside and the door swings shut, cutting off the howling wind, leaving only the sound of our ragged breathing and the pounding of my heart.

"You think you can run from me, baby girl?" he murmurs, his voice a deep rumble that goes straight to my pussy. There's a teasing edge to his words, but underneath it, I can sense something deeper. He's not just playing. He's staking a claim on me that sends a pulse of heat through my veins.

He sets me down briefly only to spin me around and lift me again, forcing my legs to wrap around his waist. The space is small and dark, the faint moonlight coming through a tiny window. We're both shivering, not only from the cold but also from the raw intensity of the moment. The air is filled with the scent of him—woodsmoke and soap, and something else, earthy and warm.

His pupils are dilated and locked on mine. There's a playful glint there, but it's mixed with something darker that sends a jolt of anticipation curling in my belly.

"I wasn't trying to run," I breathe, my voice a whisper as I lick my lips.

"Liar," he rasps.

"You're one to talk." I hold his gaze. "You're *not* a sad old man, Isaac," I say. "You're the sexiest, strongest, and most caring man I've ever met."

He pins me against the door, grabbing my face with one hand. "God, I need you, little girl," he snarls, as our lips crash together. The kiss is fierce, desperate, and frenzied.

I grind against him, aching for more friction.

He slides his hand down into my flannel pants, and inside my panties. I gasp as his fingers slip into my folds.

"*Fuck, baby,*" he groans. "You're completely drenched."

I'm already moaning as he rubs my wet pussy, his rough fingers exactly what I need. I tremble like mad, gasping and whimpering in his arms.

"You like that? How my fingers feel on your sensitive little pussy?"

"Yes, god...*yes.*" I press my head back against the door.

He bites at my neck, tracing his tongue and lips over my skin, and I arch into him.

When his fingers find my clit, my stomach clenches, the pleasure blooming up my thighs and across my hips. "Isaac! I'm going to come."

"Fuck *yes*, baby girl," he growls, then kisses me deep and hard, as his hand continues to tease at every edged nerve.

I explode, my insides like fireworks, his mouth muffling my cries.

His hand slows on my pussy but doesn't stop, drawing more gasps from me as I begin to come down.

Finally, he pulls his hand out of my panties, breaking our kiss, and sticks his two fingers in his mouth, sucking my juices off of them like it's the most delicious honey in the world.

"You taste like candy, Juniper. I can't wait to lick that sweet pussy again until you give me more of it."

"What about you?" I can feel his arousal straining in his sweats.

"No hurry," he says, holding me close, his hand on the door of the shed. "For now, let's get back to the warmth of the cabin, before we get frostbite."

As Isaac carries me, my world shifts on its axis. It's reckless and confusing, but in this moment, he's everything I want, and more.

CHAPTER 6
ISAAC

Once back in the cabin, I take Juniper to the bedroom and toss her onto the bed. Why did I even try to resist these overwhelming urges? Knowing now that she wants me as much as I want her, I'm even more ready to make her mine.

"Strip," I order, then head briefly to the bathroom. She doesn't question me, just starts to remove her clothes, her blue eyes dark with desire. It fills me with confidence, seeing her so turned on by this. By *me*.

When I return with a warm, wet washcloth, she's naked, her sweet little body nestled among the throw blankets and pillows. My cock gets even harder—which is nearly impossible, given how much it's aching already.

"You are the sexiest woman I've ever seen," I say, my voice hoarse as my eyes rove over her. "I am one lucky bastard."

I grab her cold, dirty feet and begin wiping them off with the warm cloth.

Her eyes close and she lets out a long, contented sigh. "Pretty sure I'm the lucky one, Isaac."

I can't hold back this time, replacing the washcloth with

my mouth over her tender toes. She gasps as I savor each one like a miniature popsicle.

"I wanted to do this earlier, so much," I rasp, then kiss the pads of her toes and the ball of her foot. "Your feet are adorable."

"I wouldn't have stopped you, you know," she moans, as I move to her other foot.

My lips glide over her ankle and up the inside of her calf to her knee. "Oh, I almost forgot," I say, leaning down near the side of the bed. I pull the handcuffs from my duty belt and sit back up, dangling them in front of her. "You promised you wouldn't run off again, and yet..."

I give her a playful wink as she sits up. "Whatever will you do, Sheriff?"

"I've no choice but to cuff you," I reply sternly.

"But, Sheriff..." she protests.

"It's for your own safety, Ma'am."

"*Fine*," she pouts dramatically. "If you *must*." She shoves her wrists out in front of me.

"Good girl," I say, my voice husky and raw. She visibly squirms before me. I make sure the sound of the metal locking into place around each wrist is loud and deliberate.

Grabbing the center of the cuffs, I pull her arms up and back over top of her head, at the same time pushing her body down to the bed. I stroke my hand over her tit and capture her mouth in a kiss. Then I travel down her neck and let go of the cuffs so I can caress her other breast. I tease the sensitive peak with my lips and the coarse scruff of my beard.

As I nip and lick at her pebbled nipples, she gasps and groans. When I kiss a path down her ribs and stomach, I feel her muscles clench.

"*Isaac...*" she coos as I rub my face between her thighs, inhaling her scent.

I swipe my tongue over her wet folds and she blows out a shaky breath.

"So sweet, baby girl," I groan. Then I dive deep into her pussy, exploring every secret, hidden nerve.

She cries out and arches under me. With both hands I grip her hips tight.

"I'm sorry, I wanted to go slow," I choke out, between licks and kisses. "But you taste too good, Juniper. I can't stop. I want more of you."

"I don't want you to stop, either," she keens, spreading her thighs wider and rocking her hips against my big tongue, riding it for her pleasure.

Christ, this woman.

I growl against her body, sending more vibrations through her aching little pussy. My grip tightens and I swirl my tongue around her velvety folds, wanting to draw out her orgasm as I get closer and closer to her clit.

"That feels sooooo goooood..." she moans.

"Yes..." I lap and suck gently at her sensitive bundle of nerves.

I gaze up at her as I feast on her sweetness, and watch as she spirals higher and higher, her eyes rolling back.

Her head thrashes from side to side on the pillow and her body arcs off the bed, the climax grabbing hold of her like she's possessed.

"Isaac!" she screams, her body jerking uncontrollably. I snarl, the sounds she is making bringing out the beast within me. The taste of her orgasm only gets me hungrier for her, and I lap it all up as she shakes and cries.

"Oh," she moans, drained. My thumbs brush over her skin as I slow my motions.

She's still trembling when I'm finally able to tear myself

away from her and sit up. I grin and wipe my mouth with the back of my hand. "Those cuffs hurtin' you?"

She shakes her head. "No, but I'm dying to have you inside me."

I chuckle. "Careful what you wish for, Juniper. I'm an awful big boy." I peel off my flannel, then pull my undershirt up and off. She's staring at me as I flex, puffing out my chest.

"I love how broad your shoulders are, Isaac. And that thick barrel chest, and stomach…" She bites her lip. "*Wow.*"

Emboldened by her words, I stand next to the bed and drop my sweatpants, immediately followed by my boxer briefs.

Her mouth drops open as I palm the tip of my hard-on, precum dripping out.

"You weren't kidding about being a big boy," she whispers, her eyes focused on my dick. "I'm… I'm on the pill," she stammers, then worries that sexy lip again.

"You're sure you're okay with this, Juniper?" I want her to be absolutely positive.

Her gaze lifts to mine, her eyes dancing. "Just get on top of me and fuck me already, Sheriff."

I blink, caught off guard for a moment, then smile. "Yes, Ma'am."

I climb onto her and rest my weight on her sexy body, loving the feel of her hot skin against mine. My cock is beyond hard and more than ready.

Caging her with my arms, I lean down and nuzzle her ear. "You like being my captive, being pinned down like you're my prey?"

She swallows audibly. "I do."

Goddamn, she's my ultimate fantasy.

I grin against her neck before biting down—hard enough for her to feel my teeth, but careful not to break the skin.

She moans in response.

"Tell me you're mine, little girl," I demand, shifting my weight to use my hand to guide my cock into her opening.

"Yes. Yours," she whimpers, as I push my thick member in.

"Fuck, you're so tight...I won't last long, Juniper. Hell, you'll drive me to delirium."

She chuckles, and the grip on my dick tightens. "God..." I groan.

I slide further and further into her tight, wet pussy, and her moans get louder and more insistent.

"You're so huge," she chokes out.

"Does it hurt?" Instantly I pause. "Too much for you?"

She shakes her head. "No... You're perfect."

I'm beaming on the inside. *She* is perfect.

I sit up carefully, staying inside her, and wrap her thighs around my waist.

"C'mere," I whisper, pulling her up against me and directing her to put her cuffed wrists around the back of my neck. She threads her fingers into my hair and I wrap an arm low around her ass, shoving her tight against me.

"Oh...my..." she breathes.

"Baby..."

The harder I thrust, the louder we both get. I'm thankful we're in the middle of a blizzard so no one comes knocking. I can feel every movement, every muscle she tenses, as I drive in and out of her. She's all around me, sending hot sparks to every nerve.

"*Fuck*, you're gonna kill me, Juniper," I groan. "Kill me and send me straight to Heaven."

I'm ready to fall right over the edge.

"And I'm going with you," she moans.

I grasp her face, kissing her sweet, hot mouth with everything I have. Her body suddenly jerks against me, and she breaks the kiss. "I'm coming!"

Her words have my orgasm exploding, like a massive ball of light crashing through me.

"Me too, baby. *Me too...*" I say through grit teeth. My fingers dig into her flesh as my body spasms, muscles clenching. I pump what feels like gallons of hot, sticky seed into her pussy—and she wrings every last drop from me with her vice-like grip.

We cling to each other, our hearts beating like mad next to each other. Our bodies are sweaty and slick, our hair damp.

She kisses my face, my neck, and my lips. "Yours, always," she says, between kisses, her breath still ragged.

And damn, if that isn't the best thing I've heard in a long, long time.

I wake up to an empty bed, the sheets cold beside me. Panic surges through me and I sit up, my heart racing. "Juniper?" I call out, the sound of her name echoing in the quiet room. The sudden fear is overwhelming, like a knife piercing my chest. I *can't* lose her as well. Not after Deb.

Then the bedroom door creaks open, and there she is, standing in the doorway with two steaming mugs of coffee. Her sandy blond hair is tousled, her cheeks flushed, and she's smiling—a sight that makes my chest ache for a very different reason.

"Morning," she says brightly, holding out a mug to me. "I thought you might want this."

Relief washes over me, quickly replaced by a cold, sinking feeling. I can't do this. I can't let myself care again, only to lose it all. The walls around my heart that I've carefully constructed since Deb's death slam back up. I glance out the window. The snow has finally stopped.

"Get dressed," I say, my voice harsh. "We're leaving in ten minutes."

Juniper blinks, confusion flickering in her big, blue eyes. "I made breakfast. I thought we could—"

I cut her off, swinging my legs out of bed. "Pack it up. We'll take it to go."

The hurt in her eyes is like a punch to the gut, but I force myself to ignore it. This is for the best. It's better to push her away now than to let her steal my heart completely and risk more pain.

She turns to go and soon I hear her banging around in the kitchen as I get dressed. What was I thinking last night? Pleading with her to tell me she's mine when I can't give her the same? I don't deserve her. She needs someone able to give her everything. Able to worship her like the queen she is.

The drive to her brother's house is suffocatingly silent. I can feel her eyes on me, burning into my skin, but I force myself to stare straight ahead, my grip on the steering wheel tightening with every passing second.

When I pull up to the curb, I finally muster up the courage to speak. "I'll get your car out and towed here," I say, my tone deliberately flat, as if keeping it emotionless will make it easier for both of us.

She shrugs, a small, dismissive movement that only makes the knife twist deeper in my chest. "Whatever," she says, her voice tinged with a bravado that doesn't match the glimmer of tears I catch in her eyes. It's a flash of vulnerability that's gone almost as soon as I see it, but it shatters something inside me. It's all I can do to keep myself from reaching out to her, to pull her back and tell her this isn't what I want, it's just that I'm terrified of losing her.

"Trust me, it's better this way, baby girl," I mutter under my breath, more to convince myself than her.

She freezes, her tiny hand on the door handle, before turning to me with a look that could cut through steel. "Don't you *dare*," she whispers, her voice shaking. "You are *not* allowed to call me that if you're just going to walk away."

The words are like a slap to the face. She's right. "Sorry," I reply, as I force myself to look away, unable to meet the pain in her eyes.

She just stares at me, her chest rising and falling with the weight of everything left unsaid. Then, without another word, she gets out and walks up the steps to Kyle's house, her back ramrod straight, her movements stiff.

I feel like the biggest coward in the world, every step she takes away from me an additional blow to my already crumbling resolve. The door closes behind her, and the silence that follows is deafening. I grip the steering wheel tighter, consumed by the urge to run after her, to beg her to forgive me, to admit that I'm just *scared*—scared of how much I need her, scared of how much she's come to mean to me in mere hours.

But I don't move. I sit there, paralyzed by my fear, watching the door, hoping she'll come back out, hoping I'll find the courage to do what I should have done all along. But the door remains closed, and my chance to make things right disappears.

Back at the station, I walk into my office quickly and close the door. I want to be alone, even if the silence is oppressive. I glance down at the photo of Deb on my desk. It's from before she got sick, before she wasted away to nothing. I pick it up, staring into her smiling eyes.

"What do I do, Deb?" I whisper, my voice breaking. "I don't ever want to feel pain again like I did after you died." I swallow hard, tears burning the back of my eyes. "You always said I was a big softie, too sensitive for my own damned good. Guess you were right."

I run my hand over my beard. Juniper's sweet scent is still all over me and guilt gnaws at the edges of my mind.

"I'm afraid, Deb," I murmur. "And dammit, I *know* you'd want me to move on, to find love again. Hell, you'd probably give me a swift kick in the pants right now if you were here, tell me to get my head out of my ass and do something about it."

As I put the photo back down, it slips and falls forward onto the desk. I freeze, staring at the fallen frame, half expecting Deb to pop out and give me that exasperated look she always did when I was being an idiot. My eyes widen. On the back of the frame is a large image of a crown, the brand's logo.

A crown for a queen.

"Okay, okay, message received," I say, feeling a strange sense of clarity and excitement wash over me. "I'll go get my tiny snow queen." I put the photo back upright and grin.

As I head out of the office, Deputy Barlow calls out from behind his desk. "Sheriff? Don't forget about the open Dispatch position." He nods toward the stack of applications threatening to topple over in my inbox. "We've got to start interviewing next week."

I stop in my tracks and snort. "You know," I say, glancing back at him, "I think I've already found the perfect person for the job."

CHAPTER 7
JUNIPER

I sit on the couch, doomscrolling on my phone while Kyle rattles off potential job options like he's my personal career counselor. I know he's just trying to help, but it's hard to focus. My mind keeps drifting back to Isaac.

Last night was...amazing. Best sex of my life. Honestly, best *night* of my life—even with a few hiccups. Though now I wish it hadn't been quite so great. I fell for that big ol' sheriff the moment I laid eyes on him, despite trying to convince myself otherwise. But *apparently* I'm not what he wants, long term. I'm just a silly girl with a criminal record who has a tendency to make bad decisions.

"You could take a bunch of resumes down to Main Street," Kyle suggests, bringing me back to the conversation. "See if any of the stores are hiring. Or maybe talk to Angie and T about a job at the diner." He taps the counter with his calloused fingers. "Oh! Griff over at the post office said something about wanting a change. That uniform would really bring out your eyes." He bats his eyelashes at me.

I manage a chuckle but shake my head.

"Hey, you could do worse," he continues. "At least you wouldn't have to deal with drunk idiots at a bar. Or behind it."

I nod, trying to muster up some excitement. *This is the fresh start you came to Deepwood Mountain for, girl.*

"True," I admit, my smile fading as my thoughts once again wander back to the sheriff. Damn him and his soulful brown eyes, making me feel…special. How dare he? *And* how dare he keep all my chocolate bars?!

Kyle, ever the observant brother, gives me a sidelong glance. "You okay? You seem…off. Sad, even."

I shrug, avoiding his gaze. "Just tired, I guess." It's a lame excuse, but I can't bring myself to explain everything I'm feeling inside. I can barely understand it myself. I conveniently left out most of the details when telling Kyle about last night. No need to add more complications.

Suddenly, there's a knock at the door. Kyle gets up to answer it, and I barely register the deep male voice that follows. Then Kyle's words cut through my thoughts. "Is there a problem, Sheriff? Did Junie do something wrong?"

My heart skips a beat as I see Isaac walk into the kitchen, his hat in his hands. His big form takes up most of the small space, and I hate that I like that so much. What is he doing here? My stomach churns, and my defenses immediately go up.

Isaac shakes his head, a small, reassuring smile on his lips. "No, nothing like that," he replies, his gaze locked on me, soft, almost tender.

"Juniper, could we take a walk?" he asks.

Initially, I'm too stunned to respond. Then a wave of defiance surges through me.

I get to my feet, folding my arms across my chest. "A walk? What, like we're suddenly friends now?" My voice is heavy with sarcasm.

Kyle shoots me a look, clearly taken aback by my tone. Isaac, however, doesn't flinch. He simply nods. "Yes. A walk. Please."

I huff, rolling my eyes. "Fine. Let's get this over with." I grab my coat and Isaac steps forward, ready to help me with it, but I brush him off.

"Back in a bit," I mutter to Kyle, who watches us leave with a curious, slightly concerned expression.

We step outside, the crisp air biting at my cheeks. Isaac slows his stride to stay in step beside me. The silence between us is thick and tense.

"I want to be honest with you," he finally says, as if choosing his words carefully.

I glance at him, my guard firmly up. "Oh, so *now* you want to talk to me." It comes out sharper than I intended, laced with all the hurt I've been carrying around since this morning. I can't help it; the emotional whiplash has left me reeling.

He stops walking and turns to face me. "I'm sorry," he says, "I should have handled things better. Honestly, I was scared. Scared of losing someone again, of feeling that kind of pain again." He pauses, taking a deep breath. "But the truth is, you make me feel things I thought I'd never feel again, Juniper. And that's terrifying, especially for someone who's been through what I have."

My heart softens slightly, but I'm not letting him off that easily. "You can't just show up here and say things like that after pushing me away," I snap. "Do you have any idea how confusing that is for me?"

He searches my eyes. "I can guess, yes," he admits, his voice low. "And I want to make it right."

The sincerity in his voice and the vulnerability in his eyes chip away at my defenses. He reaches out and takes my hand, and I let him. God help me, I let him. I crave his electrifying touch. "I want to live again, Juniper. Dance again. Love again. And I think it would be easy to do that with you. You'd make it easy."

His words hang in the air, a confession and a plea all at once. My heart races and my mind whirls. He brushes his thumb over my cheek, so warm, and for a second, I just let myself feel it, let myself hope, let myself believe that maybe this could work.

"I can't promise that everything will be perfect," he continues, his deep voice husky. "But I want to try. I want to worship you like the tiny queen you are. The queen of my heart."

I take a deep breath, my heart swelling with a flurry of emotions. "You're on, Sheriff," I say with a wink.

Isaac's dark brown eyes light up, a handsome smile spreading across his face. He leans down and cradles me under my ass, hauling me up against him. We kiss like two lovesick teenagers, my body wrapped around his as if we're permanently entwined.

When we finally break apart, he's still smiling. I'll never get tired of seeing that. "How about we start with a proper date?" he asks. "Tomorrow night at the Rustic Ridge?"

I raise an eyebrow, a playful grin tugging at my lips. "Sounds good. I was waiting for you to ask me out."

"I'm just not sure how long I can be out with you in public before we get hauled in for lewd conduct or indecent exposure," he teases, eyes sparkling.

I laugh, but desperately need to squeeze my thighs together at the images that pop into my head.

"But before that," he says, "I have a proposition for you."

I smile widely. "Ooh! The cuffs again?"

He grins, looking almost feral, then rolls his teeth over his lower lip. "*Not* what I was about to say, but I'll consider it for later." He chuckles. "No, a job. I think you'd be perfect for our opening in Dispatch. You know, since a lot of it is telling a bunch of officers what to do. Including me."

I blink in surprise. "You mean, I'd get to boss you around *and* be paid for it? Sounds like a dream job to me."

He laughs, squeezing my ass. "Exactly."

I nod. "I'm in!"

Before I can say anything else, his lips capture mine in a deep, possessive kiss. It feels like a taste of our future together.

I can't wait.

EPILOGUE - ISAAC
THREE YEARS LATER

I stand on the porch of our home, watching the sun set over the mountains as I rock my son Evan in my arms. Life has a way of surprising you when you least expect it, and Juniper has been the best surprise of all. She's everything to me. Since the fateful day my tiny queen burst into my life, she's changed it for the better. Her determination, her spirit, her love—they've transformed not just me, but the entire town.

After getting her 911 dispatch certification, she worked hard until she became one of the best dispatchers Deepwood Mountain has ever seen—and by extension, Hallie's best friend. The town loves her. They know her voice means help is on the way, and they trust her implicitly. And I of course love getting to hear her every day on my radio. I'm so proud of her.

I think back to those first three months when we were dating, wooing her the best way I knew—dancing at the Rustic Ridge, picnics by the lake, dinners at her favorite spots, foot massages...and flowers, always flowers. I remember proposing to her down by the lake while we were staying at the Deepwood Inn. Her eyes shimmered with tears as she said yes, and dammit if mine didn't too.

I didn't think I could get any happier—until she gave birth to our beautiful son.

These days, our two-year-old mini devil is a whirlwind of energy, just like his mama. Uncle Kyle is coming to take him for the night, giving Juniper and me some much-needed "alone time". I have been aching for her for what feels like *forever*...

Kyle arrives, and after a flurry of hugs and reminders about snacks and bedtime routines, he heads off with our little boy. Juniper stands next to me, an arm wrapped around my waist, her head on my chest. I slide my hand down her back.

"Better run, little girl," I rasp, grabbing a handful of her luscious ass.

She yelps and instantly takes off in a mad dash toward the forest that encloses our house. I give her a moment before I'm off and chasing after her.

The thrill hits me instantly, primal and raw, my pulse quickening as I watch her disappear between the trees. The air is alive with the scent of fresh earth, the ground still soft from a recent rain. Spring has woken everything up, including the wildness that lives inside me when it comes to Juniper. She's fast, but I know these woods like the back of my hand, and there's no way I'm letting her get away from me.

The forest closes around us, the sunlight filtering through the budding leaves and casting dappled shadows on the ground. I can hear her laughter echoing through the trees, light and teasing, urging me to pick up the pace. The hunt is on, and she knows it.

I dodge low-hanging branches, my boots pounding the soft earth as I wind through the trees, the cool air rushing past my face. Her figure is just ahead, a blur of motion as she tries to put more distance between us. I can see the determination in her every move, the playful defiance in the way she tosses glances back at me, daring me to close the gap.

"I'm coming for you, baby," I call out, my voice a mix of amusement and the desperation that makes my groin throb whenever I'm near her.

She just laughs, a sound that's half-challenge, half-invitation. It only spurs me on. The chase is as much a game as it is a dance—a dance we've perfected over time, where the thrill of the hunt is matched only by the sweet satisfaction of the capture.

She weaves through the trees with an agility that only makes me want her more. My eyes lock on her like a predator targeting its prey, my every sense attuned to the rhythm of her movements and the sound of her breath.

I push harder, my muscles burning as I get closer. The forest goes hazy around me, my attention fixed solely on her. I'm close now—close enough to see the way her shoulders tense up when she realizes how near I am.

With a final burst of speed, I lunge forward, my hand brushing against her arm as she tries to veer to the side. But I'm ready, anticipating the move, and I wrap an arm around her waist, pulling her back against me with a growl that's as full of laughter as it is triumph. "Gotcha."

She gasps, struggling playfully in my grip, but there's no real fight in it, just the last bit of resistance before her surrender. "You're getting faster," she teases, breathless, a grin in her tone.

"And you're as slippery as ever," I reply, pulling her closer, feeling the warmth of her body against mine. There's something intoxicating about hunting her, having her here, caught in my arms, knowing she's mine—forever.

I turn her toward a fallen pine tree, push her forward, and

kick her feet apart. "Now bend over that tree, baby girl, so I can fuck you from behind."

"Christ," she groans, her ass in the air.

I pull her sundress up to see she's not wearing any panties and my cock rages even more.

"Where *are* your panties, baby girl?" I ask, spanking her ass cheek. She gasps.

"Dunno," she answers sassily. "Lost 'em, I guess."

I spank her other cheek before running my hands up her trembling thighs. She's so eager for me and what I'm about to do to her, it's driving me crazy.

She's already sopping wet when I reach around and slide my fingers into her softness. She moans as I rub her pussy in slow circles, teasing her clit. "God yes, right there," she cries out.

I rub faster, too hard to be able to take my time with her, and grind against her ass. Within seconds she detonates, a shaking, convulsing orgasm ripping through her.

Moments later my pants are down around my ankles, and I'm thrusting into her still-spasming pussy. "*Fuck me*, sweet girl," I roar as I fill her up. The tight, hot grip of her channel is too much, and I pump fast and hard against her, knowing my cock is ready to explode...

Now.

"*Juniper*!!!" I yell into the canopy of trees, as my climax tears through my body. I hold onto her as if my life depended on it, and my legs nearly give out as I fill her with my seed.

My sweet little hellion screams out my name as another orgasm crashes over her.

Her breath comes in quick, panting bursts as she begins to come down. It matches the way my heart pounds, the way my blood thrums in my veins.

The forest around us seems to hold its breath, the world

narrowing to just the two of us, locked in a game that neither of us wants to end. The excitement of the hunt, the satisfaction of the capture and the joy of the release—it's all there, a heady mix that leaves me thoroughly content every time.

But for now, I savor the feel of her hips in my hands, and the wild, untamed connection that binds us together.

Eventually we stroll back toward the house, hand in hand, following the familiar path winding through the trees. The world feels hushed, the only sounds the crunch of leaves underfoot and the distant call of birds bedding down for the night.

"Isaac," Juniper says, breaking the peaceful silence. "I love our life. I love you."

I stop and turn to her, taking her hands in mine. "I love you too, Juniper. More than I ever thought possible. You've given me everything—hope, happiness, a family. I can't imagine life without you."

She steps closer, her eyes shining. "I'm pregnant again."

I blink, speechless, the joy welling up inside me almost too much to contain. Then I laugh, a deep, happy sound, and pull her into my arms. "You've made me the happiest man in the world," I whisper, my heart overflowing. "Is it okay for me to say I hope we have a girl this time?"

"Ooh, I think so," she says, grinning up at me. "Pretty sure they come with the same amount of diapers. You still have diaper duty, by the way."

"Fair enough," I chuckle, kissing the top of her head. "Promise you'll let me name her?"

She arches an eyebrow suspiciously. "If it's something ridiculous, I reserve the right to veto."

"Fine," I say, smiling as my mind turns with all the potential names. "How about we start with something simple, like...Ethel?"

"*Ethel*? What are we having, a reincarnated 80-year-old woman?" She swats my arm playfully. "You can do better than that, Sheriff."

"Gertrude?"

"Don't Reece and Paige have a pig named Gertrude at the sanctuary?" She purses her lips.

"Good point," I say, scratching my jaw. "How about… Delilah?"

She blinks. "That's…actually really pretty. I like it."

I rest my hand on her belly. "Delilah Quinn."

"Perfect," she says with a grin.

"Sure is," I reply, with more hope and love in my heart than I ever thought possible.

~

Want to read more from Husky Valley?
Check out the **Husky Valley** series page:
https://www.lexihayes.com/series/husky-valley
Need to catch up with the main Deepwood Mountain books?
Check out the **Deepwood Mountain** series page:
https://www.lexihayes.com/series/deepwood-mountain

You can sign up for my newsletter via my website:
www.lexihayes.com
It's the best way to hear about new and upcoming releases,
plus get access to subscriber exclusives and bonus content.

And as always, if you liked this story, please post a review on any of your preferred platforms. Reviews are the lifeblood of independent authors like me, and I welcome your opinions and feedback.
Thanks for reading!

TEASED BY THE MAILMAN

CHAPTER 1
GRIFF

The door chimes cheerfully as I step into Stevie's Salon, the sound instantly chasing away the monotony of my day so far.

The place is a riot of colors and scents, all competing for a visitor's attention. The walls are decorated with vibrant and unusual artwork, while the air is thick with the aroma of shampoos, sprays, and nail polish, a heady mix of fresh citrus and tangy florals. Everything feels alive, from the buzz of the clippers to the happy chatter that bounces around the room over the darkwave music.

I feel very out of place in my postal uniform, the blue shorts, button down shirt and ball cap a far cry from the goth/alt aesthetic of those working here. I'm also hyper aware of the extra pounds straining my shirt around my midsection.

Mathias hurries over in black everything, a stack of folded towels in his hands. "You can just leave the mail there, Griff, thanks." He motions to the reception desk near the door with his long, thin fingers, adorned with many silver rings.

I set the mail down on the counter. "I'm getting a cut today, too," I say, before he has a chance to run off.

His charcoal-lined eyes snap to the clock on the wall. "*My god*, 12:30 already? Where has the day gone?" His gaze moves to Stevie, who's laughing with a young blonde woman in her chair. "She'll be with you just as soon as she finishes with Juniper," he says.

Ah, right, the Sheriff's wife. I thought she looked familiar.

I thank him, instantly drawn to Stevie like an industrial strength magnet to sheet metal. She's in her element, slender hands moving deftly and artfully as she primps Juniper's curls. Her own hair, cut short and currently dyed a rich shade of violet, shines under the overhead lights. The color complements the glinting rows of metal rings and studs that line the shell of her ears. A tight black band T-shirt fits snug against her sweet little tits, and the micro mini skirt showing off her snow-white legs and rainbow of tattoos has me thinking dirty thoughts already. I swallow hard, my heart racing, feeling the familiar flutter of longing that always comes with a side order of disbelief. Every time I see her, I'm struck by how much I'm attracted to her—both her sexy little body and her playful energy.

"Yo, big hunk o' mailman!" she calls, bringing me back to the moment. Mathias puts down the towels to take Juniper's payment after Stevie gives her a hug goodbye, and then Stevie's eyes lock onto mine.

Shit. How does she do that? Make me feel as if I'm the only one in the room?

I remove my ball cap, ruffling my hair as she walks up to me.

Her glossy red lips split into a wide grin. "Those luscious locks of yours are just begging for some TLC, Teddy Bear."

"Well, you know you're the only one who can tame them properly, Pixie Pie," I say, giving her a wink. I swear, I become a different person when she's around. Flirty. Fun. Sexually charged. And I like it.

I gave her the nickname Pixie Pie long ago, when she was just a kid. Her big brother Harris and I have been best friends since elementary school, and we were already teenagers by the time Stevie came along. She's always looked like a little pixie to me.

She chuckles and motions for me to follow her back to the washing stations. Her cute hips sway back and forth in front of me and I desperately try to keep myself in check. "You're looking thin, Pixie Pie. After we're done here can I bring you a pizza? Or a burger from Marge's? I'll still be on my lunch break."

She rolls her eyes as I settle into one of the chairs, and she drapes the salon cape over me, velcroing it around my neck. The brush of her nails on my neck sends shivers throughout my body, and my groin tightens.

Thank god for loose salon capes, is all I'm saying.

"Thanks for your concern, Griff," she says, with the light press of her hand to tip me back before she turns on the water. "But I have a perfectly good turkey sandwich on rye and bag of chips I packed for myself to have as soon as I'm done with you."

"Okay," I say, and try to relax, but the anticipation of her hands running through my hair sends my mind into a wild spiral. I've been coming to her to get my hair cut since she opened the place years ago, yet every touch always feels electric, like the first flush of warmth after too long in the cold.

"The water temp okay for you?" she asks, but her fingers are now touching my scalp and I'm having a hell of time finding my voice.

"Mmm-hmm," I croak.

The sudden intimacy is jolting and downright erotic. I can't stop myself from letting out a groan from the way her hands are rubbing and massaging sensuously and tugging at my hair.

My cock goes as hard as a steel pole in my shorts.

"Good?" she says near my ear.

Not good. Fucking amazing…

"Bliss," I answer, on a shaky breath.

She doesn't reply, just continues to drive me crazy, her nails drawing patterns on my scalp. Is it wrong that I could come without too much more of this? Probably. In fact, I *have* come picturing this very scenario, working myself over with my fist late at night, imagining Stevie's tight little body naked, her talented hands starting in my hair, then moving down to massage…other things.

The way she smiles at me—almost knowingly?—makes me forget all my insecurities and all the other reasons I can't cross the line, if only for a fleeting moment.

"Come on. Time to get that forest up there under control." I don't even realize she's finished washing my hair. I shake myself out of my stupor and follow her to her station, settling into the plush chair.

Stevie picks up the scissors, her focus laser sharp as she approaches. I gulp, feeling an insane thrill at her closeness once again.

"Just sit back and let me work my magic," she says, her voice silky and teasing.

I feel myself nodding, but the cat has got my tongue once again. The tongue I desperately want to use to trace that tattoo of a hummingbird on the underside of her arm while she giggles and squirms—*down, boy*.

I'm truly entranced by the skillful way she handles the tools of her trade. She's mesmerizing. The ache inside me only keeps growing, twisting in my chest. It's a lost cause. Why would someone like her ever be interested in a big oaf like me? Not to mention, Harris would kill me if he knew how much I wanted his little sister. I'm big, but he's bigger, and stronger… and *my best goddamned friend*. Why can't I buck these feelings?

Just as she's separating sections of my hair and trimming them, a loud buzz vibrates in my pocket. I shift to pull it out of my shorts and get it out over the cape. I glance at the screen. Harris—of course.

"You mind if I take this? It's your big bro," I tell Stevie. "He probably wants to tell you to eat something, too."

She huffs playfully and punches my bicep. "Oh my god, you guys! I eat plenty!"

I let my gaze rake over her deliberately. "I might need some proof of that."

She throws up her hands. "Answer your damn phone, or Harris is going to shit a brick."

I smirk and answer with a quick tap. "What's up, numb nuts?"

Stevie giggles next to me, then grabs a broom and starts sweeping up around the chair.

"Shut up, ass munch," Harris growls on the other end of the line.

"I'm getting my hair cut. Make it quick."

"Sure thing," he says. "Finley and I decided to celebrate our anniversary by going camping up at Glacier Rim for a few days." An audible smile warms his voice. "We want you to join us."

"On your anni—"

"And tell Stevie to come, too," he interrupts. "I'm sure she needs a break. She works too much."

I blink, my mouth suddenly dry. The thought of spending time in the wilderness with Stevie—tangled in sleeping bags, sharing laughter around a campfire, getting lost in the depths of her wicked hazel eyes—is tempting, but it also stirs up a swirling vortex of panic.

I cast a nervous look her way, wondering if she can hear her brother. She's fiddling with a pair of scissors and forcing a very deliberate nonchalance while chewing on her full bottom lip—*damn it*!

"I dunno, Harris."

"Come on, Griff. What, you have to stay late at work to organize stamps or somethin'?"

"You're a riot," I reply, shaking my head.

"Look, Finley misses her bestie, and you're the only one I trust to bring Stevie. Her car's no good at rough terrain. Besides, you know her sense of direction is shit."

He has a point. Stevie's sedan is old and unreliable, and cute as she is, without GPS she drives around in circles.

"Besides, I've missed ya, buddy. It's been a while since we've hung out together. I wanna start making up for all those years I spent away from Deepwood Mountain. Away from my family and friends—"

"Sheesh, way to hit me in the feels," I sigh. "Fine, I'll come! And I'll bring Stevie with me."

Stevie stops sweeping and looks at me.

"You're the best!" Harris says. "Now get back to your haircut, softie. And give my little sister a big sloppy kiss from me, will ya?" He laughs and hangs up, leaving me blushing thinking about "sloppy kissing" Stevie.

Such a butthead.

As I hang up the phone, Stevie flashes a curious smile, peering at me from beneath her thick lashes. "Where are you taking me?" she asks, and I melt.

Anywhere you damn well want, baby.

"Camping," I mutter, my heart thumping frantically. "He

wants me to—uh, he wants *us* to go camping with him and Finley at Glacier Rim this weekend."

"Camping?" she repeats excitedly. "That sounds amazing! I haven't seen Finley in like forever. And yeah, I guess it would be nice to see my brother, too." She gives me a wink.

When I don't respond right away she says, "You don't seem thrilled, Griff." Her penetrating eyes study me, her lips twitching up into an amused smirk as she goes back to trimming my hair. "What's a big guy like you afraid of?"

I snort. "You know what your brother's like. He can be a bit...much...when it comes to camping. Sometimes I just want to chill with a beer, not take a ten-mile hike up the biggest mountain he can find."

She laughs, a sound that thrums low in my belly.

"Well then we'll just stay by the fire and eat s'mores," she offers, a bright light twinkling in her eyes. "I'm the reigning champion for the number of marshmallows I can fit in my mouth, did you know that?"

Ergh. I chuckle uneasily. I really don't need the image of Stevie stuffing things in her mouth in my head right now.

"There'll be bugs," I say, trying to change the subject.

"Oh my god, seriously? You have nothing to worry about there. I make an all-natural bug repellent lotion that is primo." She sprays a little mousse into her hands and begins styling my hair in the mirror.

"Really? Cool."

"Yeah. Mathias gave me the recipe. It's moisturizing and smells great too. I can rub it anywhere you think the bugs might get you."

Oh god. I clear my suddenly thick throat. "Uh—really."

"C'mon, Griff, it'll be fun," She nudges my arm, the warmth of her touch causing my pulse to race. "Just think about it—wiener cookouts, watching the stars, telling horror stories around the campfire."

Wiener. I grunt. "That does sound fun. But you'll steer clear of wild animals, right? Harris told me about the time you tried to befriend a mountain lion."

"Leo was just a little grumpy that day," she says, grinning in mock innocence, readying the hair dryer. "Don't worry, I'll stay out of trouble—at least, I'll try."

She winks as she turns on the dryer. I'm grinning like a fool, enjoying her playful spirit.

Once my hair is dry she ends with a quick trim of my beard. It's borderline torture when she runs her fingers through it. But eventually she's done, and applies finishing spray to both my hair and beard.

She finally rips away the cape. Thankfully, I've managed to will my erection away enough that I don't embarrass myself. Then she slides her hands over my shoulders, gazing at me in the mirror.

"Much better, Griff—if I do say so myself." She brushes the back of my collar and leans down near my ear. "Pretty hot, too."

I chuckle, getting up from the chair. "Thanks, but you don't have to do that, Pixie Pie."

Her brow furrows. "Do what?"

"Patronize me." I turn to head to the front to pay, but she grabs my wrist, stopping me.

The feel of her fingers on my arm is electric.

"I am *not* patronizing you. You *are* a hottie, Griff Pierce," she declares, standing in front of my six-foot-four frame, tilting her head back to glare at me. She looks angry, for some reason.

I… I don't know what to say in return.

She licks her lips. "So, what time are you picking me up tomorrow?"

The lip thing has me so flustered that I've forgotten what she's talking about. What are we doing tomorrow, again?

Oh!

"Uh...10 AM?"

"Perf! I'll bring some snacks and drinks," she says with a smile. "Bye, Griff." She turns back to her station, and Mathias waves me over.

Wait.

Did Stevie Nolan just call me a hottie?

CHAPTER 2
STEVIE

"Jeezus! I'm a hot mess!" I announce to my empty room.

The sun streams through the windows of my apartment, spotlighting the chaos I've created. Clothes are strewn across the bed, an unholy mismatch of colors and styles. Camping gear is scattered on the floor, and I'm standing in the middle of it all, chewing my lip as I debate what to pack.

I'm not used to feeling this nervous or anxious about *anything*. Certainly not clothes.

I'm usually the confident, quirky, fun-loving artsy one, but right now, I feel as lost and vulnerable as a kid on their first day at a new school.

I catch a glimpse of myself in the mirror, my hair a spiky mess of purple tangles from running my hands through it. I take a deep breath, steadying myself. My reflection stares back at me, the rings and studs lining my ears and the curved barbell in my navel glinting in the light. Combined with the tattoos that decorate my arms, legs, and midsection, the jewelry is a visual reminder of the boldness that almost always comes naturally to me.

But this is different. This is *Griff*.

As in, the man I've had a crush on for ages. Since I was old enough to have these kind of feelings.

My mind drifts back to the salon and the way Griff's muscles tensed under my touch while I washed his hair. The groan that escaped his lips sent such a shiver down my spine that I found myself suddenly wanting to do much more than just massage his scalp. I wanted to trace the lines of his body, feel the smoothness of his skin under my fingertips.

I shake my head, snapping myself out of my daydream. *Focus on packing, girl.* I grab a flannel shirt, folding it neatly before placing it in my bag. Then my mind wanders again, remembering the way Griff's gaze lingered on me, the warmth in his eyes when he laughed at my jokes yesterday. There were moments when I could swear there was more to his teasing, a spark of something deeper. But at the time I brushed it off like I always do, chalking it up to wishful thinking.

I'm just his best friend's little sister. Way too young not to mention weird for a big, brawny mountain man with simple tastes.

I pack my homemade bug repellent. The thought of rubbing the lotion onto his skin, of feeling his body respond to my touch... It's enough to make my panties wet all over again.

I glance at the clock. Crap, I need to hurry. I stuff the rest of my clothes into my bag, not bothering to fold them. I can sort that all out later. Right now, I need to pull myself together.

The Montana morning air is crisp and fresh as I step outside my apartment. I love this time of year, summer melting away to fall, the leaves starting to change, a slight chill in the breeze at times. It's perfect camping weather—*and cuddling weather.* But I'm not going to think about that. *Nope, nope, nope.*

Griff's truck rumbles into view, a beast of a vehicle that

suits its owner perfectly. My heart skips a beat as he pulls up to the curb, his newly trimmed hair shining in the light. He looks good—like, *really* good. I love the way his flannel shirt stretches across his broad chest and the way his arms fill out the sleeves. *Hottie,* just like I told him yesterday.

He gets out of the truck, his eyes scanning me from head to toe. I suddenly feel self-conscious, wondering if I'm dressed warmly enough. Our eyes meet, and I could swear there's something different there. Or is it my imagination?

"Morning, Pixie Pie," he says, his voice husky. I wonder if that's how he sounds right when he first wakes up.

Oh my. My cheeks heat. *Ahem.*

"Morning, Teddy Bear," I reply, a smirk playing on my lips, trying to tamp those thoughts down.

He grabs my bags, effortlessly swinging them into the back of the truck. I climb into the passenger seat, taking in the interior. I've never actually been in his truck. It's clean and well-maintained, which doesn't surprise me at all. A forest-scented air freshener dangles from the rearview mirror, filling the cab with a fresh, piney aroma.

I turn to Griff as he slides into the driver's seat, his large frame making the truck seem smaller all of a sudden. "Want something to drink? I brought coffee, hot chocolate, and water. And some snacks—chips, veggies, fruit?"

He glances at me, a soft smile on his face. "Just water, thanks."

I twist around to pull out a bottle from the cooler directly behind me and hand it to him before taking a sip of my coffee. I watch as he drinks, the muscles in his throat working as he swallows. It's strangely mesmerizing, and I find it hard to look away.

Once he's pulled onto the road, I open a bag of carrot sticks.

"Hey, check it out. I'm eating." I crunch the carrot with a dramatic flourish as soon as he glances my way.

He smirks. "Carrot sticks? Please. I want to see you eat something deep fried or gooey as fuck."

I laugh. "I told you: I'll be eating tons of s'mores."

"You'd better, or I'll have to hold you down and force them into your mouth."

An image pops unbidden into my head of Griff forcing *something* into my mouth—and baby, it ain't s'mores.

I need to change the subject.

"So... I hear you're looking for a change in career or something."

He chuckles. "Man, you can't say anything to people in this town without it getting around."

"Jeez, are you new here?" I ask, rolling my eyes and snapping another carrot stick in half.

He levels his gaze at me.

"Is it a huge secret?" I press him. "Because Juniper mentioned it yesterday in passing."

"No, no secret, I guess. I was chatting with her brother Kyle when I delivered mail to McCafferty Customs the other day..."

"What are you thinking? Or do you not know yourself yet?"

He's quiet for a moment, his fingers tapping the steering wheel. "I'm not sure," he finally says. "I guess I'd like to own a business. Like, a brick-and-mortar store. Something to be proud of that I can pass on to my kids someday."

I tuck that nugget of information away, a seed of an idea planting itself in my mind. My dad's made noises about selling the general store. Maybe Griff would be interested in taking it over.

"I'd miss you stopping by the salon every day." *And seeing him in that tight uniform.* "But that's awesome," I say, my voice soft. "You should go after what you want, Griff. Whatever makes you happy."

He glances at me, his eyes lingering longer than usual. I start to sweat.

"Thanks, Pixie Pie," he finally says, taking another drink of water and returning his eyes to the road. "Just so you know, I'd miss seeing you every day, too. But I'd still come every month for my haircut."

I grin. "What if you decide to grow it out, like Harris? And let your beard get as long as his? You'll run off to join a ZZ Top cover band and I'll never see you again!"

He laughs, a deep rumbling sound that fills the cab. "You know I can't pull off your brother's look. He's a lot cooler than me."

"Highly debatable," I say, shaking my head.

"I can barely manage my beard as it is. I'm always getting shit in it and struggling to keep it clean." He frowns. "Sorry, Pixie Pie, you're stuck. You'll be cutting my hair until I don't have any left to cut."

I laugh, but inside I'm thrilled.

"What about you? More tattoos? More piercings?" He gives me a stern look. "We've established you're not allowed to change careers without seriously screwing up my life."

"I guess I'm stuck too then," I tease. "Nah, no more piercings for me. Maybe more ink." I open the cooler and grab a water, then take a sip. "For the salon...I'm considering expanding. I've got the space, and I think it makes sense to add a couple more talented stylists. Our little town is growing, right?"

Griff smiles, looking at me as if genuinely interested. It makes me want to share more, to open up in a way I haven't with anyone else except maybe Finley.

"I also have a secret project," I whisper conspiratorially.

"Oh?" He arches a brow.

"Yeah. I want to start a line of men's hair care products inspired by the natural beauty of Deepwood Mountain. *For the rugged mountain man in you.* That's the tagline I've been playing around with. You like?"

Griff chuckles. "Impressive." He shakes his head. "You never cease to amaze me, Stevie. You're interesting. Unique. Creative, and a smart businesswoman too. I admire that. I'm not creative by any means. One day I'll have to pick your brain about all that stuff and take notes."

My heart swells. His words make me feel seen: sometimes I feel like my inner self is overlooked *because* of how different I look on the outside.

"You're sweet, Griff. But creativity is not always innate. Sometimes you have to work at it, like a muscle."

"Maybe you can help me train, then," he says, and I smile.

I wink. "Anytime."

After a couple of hours we stop for lunch at a burger joint and to stretch our legs briefly. But we're making good time and are eager to get back on the road. Soon the landscape changes, becoming more rugged and remote, the sun slowly dipping below the horizon.

I'm watching the light fade through the tall trees out my window when Griff curses under his breath. The truck lists to one side and warning light pops up on his dash.

"What's that?" I ask.

He grumbles. "Probably a flat tire."

"Uh oh."

My heart beats a little faster as Griff pulls over to the side of the road. The seclusion of our location adds an edge of urgency to the situation. He gets out to assess the damage, leaving me with a tantalizing view of his broad back in the right side mirror as he squats down.

I crack my door open. "I can help, you know."

He twists to look at me. "I know. But I want you to stay safe inside the truck. Okay?"

"Fine," I sigh, closing my door. I watch him work, the light casting long shadows across his face. He's all business, his movements efficient and deliberate. It's sexy as hell, and I find myself biting my lip to keep from cat-calling. Or saying something I might regret.

"Are you fucking kidding me?" I hear him yell.

I lean out the window to see what's wrong. "What is it?"

He looks up at me, a frustrated expression on his face. "The spare is flat, too."

CHAPTER 3
GRIFF

Darkness presses down over the fiery orange lines of the sky. The jagged peaks of the mountains loom in the distance, their silhouettes blending more and more with the gathering night. The rugged beauty of the Montana wilderness is breathtaking, but the isolation is palpable. The road stretches out, empty and endless, a lifeline to civilization that feels impossibly far away now.

Dammit. I should've checked the spare before we left, but Stevie had me all knotted up inside. I could barely think of anything except her as I prepared for the trip. I'm lucky I was able to dress myself properly knowing I'd be spending the drive with her and her alone.

I curse under my breath as I stare at the busted tire, frustration and helplessness washing over me like a cold tide. I'm used to having a plan, a solution, but right now, all I have is a flat and no way to fix or replace it. I glance back at Stevie, gazing at me wide-eyed through the window, and a surge of protectiveness roars through me. She's counting on me, and I can't let her down.

"All right, Pixie Pie," I say, climbing back into the truck. "Here's the deal. If you haven't noticed, we're in the middle of nowhere and cell reception is pretty spotty. I saw a gas station a few miles back, but it's getting late and I doubt they're still open. We could contact Harris and Finley and see if they can have someone nearby come out, but again, even if we can get through to them, it's late. Everything closes early in these parts."

Stevie blinks. "Are you saying we're stranded for the night?"

I tip my head back and forth. "Well, there *are* other options. They just aren't ideal." I quickly add, "Not that being stranded here is ideal, of course, but—"

"Cool, an adventure!" Stevie's lips curl into a half-smile, her face lighting up.

I chuckle. *This girl is fucking amazing.* A warmth spreads through my chest, mixed with the awe and affection I feel for her that's become so familiar these days. "That's one way of looking at it," I reply. "So... Are you saying you'd rather spend the night in the truck and walk to the station in the morning?"

She nods. "For sure. As long as we let Harris and Finley know we're okay."

"I'll try texting."

"Sounds like a plan, Teddy Bear. Let's make the most of it." She says that in her silky, sultry voice, and *Christ* is it a cock tease.

It's already been hell keeping my thoughts from traveling down that path.

With that cropped sweater she's wearing that shows off her flat, pale stomach and silver belly piercing, I had to bat away terrible ideas of flicking my tongue into her sexy navel. And those tiny cut off jean shorts? Those should be illegal.

I start the engine to keep the heater running for Stevie's sake, but as for me, I'm burning up.

"How about a little picnic?" she asks.

"Why not?" I reply.

She gathers snacks from the cooler and then flips open a secret compartment.

"You brought beer?" I say, spotting a six pack of cans.

She laughs, and shrugs. "Hey, you never know when you'll need it."

"You planned so much better than I did," I laugh, as she sets out a spread between us.

"Not another word." She puts her finger up as a warning.

I chuckle, and soon the hiss of the beer cans opening fills the cab.

"I guess this is as good a time as any to tell you," she begins, ripping open a chip bag as I take a sip of my drink. "My dad wants to sell his store."

I nearly spit out my beer. "What?"

She hands me a napkin from her purse, and continues: "He's been running it for decades, you know? It's been his whole life. But he's getting older, and now that Zoe's busy running her own Christmas shop, he's realizing it's probably time for him to retire." She sighs, picking at the tab on her beer can. "He wants to sell it, but not to just anyone. It's more than a store to him—it's his legacy."

I nod. "That's a big decision. What do you think he'll do?"

She shrugs, a small smile playing over her lips. "I think he's hoping to sell to someone who loves the store as much as he does. Someone who can keep its soul alive."

Her eyes meet mine, and I see the unspoken question in them. I take a deep breath, the words tumbling out before I can stop them. "I love that store too, Stevie. I've always loved it. And I think... Wow, you've given me a lot to think about."

Her eyes shine with excitement. "Really, Griff? You'll think about it?"

I chuckle, the idea taking root in my mind. "Honestly, I don't know that I really have to think. It would be an honor. And owning my own business would make me feel steadier. Established, you know? Like it was time to find a woman who'd put up with me, maybe even start a family."

Stevie's eyes go soft for a moment. Then she shakes it off and tsks. "That's a tall order. I mean, what woman would want a teddy bear?" She rolls her eyes.

"You don't have to tell me how difficult it'll be for me to find someone." I down the rest of my beer and crush the can in my hand viciously.

"You know, as much as I like to tease you, Griff... You're a catch! Ruggedly hot, too." She reaches out and touches my knee.

Time stops.

Stevie is touching my knee, we're alone in the truck, *and* she just called me hot. Again. Twice in two days! Am I dreaming?

"Kind, funny, strong. And I..."

She trails off. I wait for her to continue, but she just stares at her hand on my knee.

"And you what?" I ask.

She lifts her gaze to mine.

"I'm...um...kinda cold. Do you have a blanket?"

"Oh. Yeah. I have a couple in the back." I have a feeling that wasn't what she was about to say *at all*, but I can't dwell on that now. I get out of the cab and go around to open the back of the vehicle. The topper over the truck bed has kept our things warm and dry and I pull out a couple of blankets.

I open the passenger door and wrap the fuzzier one around

Stevie, rubbing her arms. "There ya go," I say, before walking around and getting in on my side.

"Better?" I ask.

"Much." She smiles at me and removes her boots. "Thanks."

I nod. "You bet."

The mood in the truck has shifted somehow. I can feel her tension and I'm worried.

"Griff, there's something I need to tell you."

My heart races, my pulse pounding in my ears. Fuck, she's going to tell me she's met someone or that I'm making her feel uncomfortable or something, I just know it. A dark sense of impending doom settles over me. "Yeah?" is the best I can come up with. Fantastic, Griff. That's some eloquence right there.

Her fingers play with the hem of the blanket. "Yeah. I don't want to make things awkward, and I'm sure you only think of me as Harris's weird little sister who cuts your hair every month, but..." She bites her lip and looks up at me. "I've had a crush on you," she whispers, her voice soft but steady, "for as long as I can remember."

Boom.

Her words hang in the air between us. I stare at her, my mind a tornado of emotions. Shock, disbelief, and a terrifying sense of joy bubbles up from deep within me. I've dreamed of hearing these words, but never thought I would.

I open my mouth to respond, but the words get caught in my throat. I'm afraid of saying them, of the consequences that could follow. But as I look into Stevie's eyes, I see a vulnerability that mirrors my own, a raw honesty that demands an equally honest response.

Then she's crumbling. "Oh god, you're not saying

anything. I'm sorry, Griff. I'm so sorry. I shouldn't have said anything. Wow, you must really think I'm crazy."

"Stevie," I finally manage to choke out, grabbing her arm. "Pixie Pie, I have a crush on you, too. I've wanted to tell you for so long, but I was always scared of ruining our friendship and of what Harris might say...and, okay, maybe a little freaked out about what he'd do to me."

Her eyes widen, a mixture of surprise and relief washing over her lovely face. "Really?"

I nod, the weight of my confession lifting from my shoulders. "I've been in love with you for years. But you're so young, so cool, so put together—way out of my league. Hell, you own a successful business! I'm just a chonky mailman. I never dreamed you would want someone like me."

She reaches out and grasps my hand in both of hers, the warmth of her touch sending a jolt of electricity through me. "Griff, you're amazing exactly how you are. Big and sexy and rugged. I *love* that you're a mailman." She giggles. "Though I'd be happy if you switched it up and owned the general store. You're everything I've ever wanted."

Her words fill me with a sense of wonder and disbelief. I've spent so long believing I wasn't good enough, that I couldn't compare to the beautiful, unique creature that is Stevie Nolan. But now, as I look into her hazel eyes, I see a side of myself reflected in them that I've never seen before—a man who is worthy and who is loved.

The realization hits me like a physical blow, a wave of emotion sweeping through me and leaving me breathless. She brings my hand up to cup her cheek, her porcelain skin smooth and soft beneath my touch.

The urge to possess her is overwhelming, a primal need that roars through me like wildfire. I lean over the center console, pulling her face toward me, my lips capturing hers. She tastes like beer and salt and everything sweet.

Her hands come up to tangle in my hair, her fingers sliding through the strands as she pulls me closer. The kiss deepens, our tongues stroking and exploring, an explosion of sensation that leaves me dizzy.

I pull back, my breath coming in ragged gasps as I meet her gaze. Her eyes are dark with desire, her cheeks flushed. "Stevie," I whisper, my voice rough with need. "I want you so badly. But I don't want to come between you and your brother. I couldn't live with myself if I messed up your relationship."

"That's fair," she says. "But I need you, Griff. Even if it's just for tonight."

I sigh. "If that's what you want. You know I'd give you anything, Stevie...but it's gonna kill me to not be able to call you mine tomorrow."

She nods and blows out a breath. "Yeah..."

My thumb strokes over her lush lips. "I need to be closer to you, Stevie," I growl.

Her eyes drift closed for a moment. "Let's get in the back."

"You sure?"

She kisses my thumb. "Yep. Completely sure."

I reluctantly let her go and get out of the cab, running around to her side, pulling her into my arms and carrying her into the back. It's cold, but I hustle, spreading out the sleeping bags and our blankets.

She pulls me toward her, making room for me to explore. I run my hands over her body, tracing the intoxicating curves of her waist, her hips, her thighs. She shivers under my touch, her breath hitching as I trail my fingers up the smooth, flat plane of her belly.

I lift her sweater, revealing the curve of her sweet little tits in a delicate black lace bra. I lean down, pressing a kiss to her skin, already addicted to the taste of her. She arches into my touch, a soft moan escaping her as I unhook the front clasp of her bra, freeing her breasts.

I take one pebbled nipple into my mouth, my tongue swirling around the sensitive peak as she gasps, her hips writhing against me. I trail kisses down her stomach, pausing a moment to nibble on her navel, my tongue flicking over the piercing.

"That's so nice…" she moans.

While I lick her belly stud, my hands tug at the waistband of her shorts, eager to reveal more of her body. She lifts her hips, helping me slide the denim down her legs, revealing the tiny black thong.

"Oh, Stevie…these panties just aren't fair," I groan, running my fingers over the soaked fabric, the heat of her pussy scorching. She shivers, her breath ragged, as I slip my fingers into the thong, finding her slick and ready. I stroke her gently, sliding along her velvety skin, my thumb circling her clit as she moans, her head falling back against the seat.

The sight of her spread out before me, lost in pleasure, is almost more than I can bear. I pull off her panties and dip my head, my mouth replacing my fingers as I taste her sweet, wet, needy pussy. Damn, she tastes like heaven.

"Griff!" Her hands spear through my hair as I lick and suck, my tongue exploring every inch of her sensitive core.

Her hips buck against my mouth, her breath coming hard and fast as she chases her release. I focus on her clit, my tongue swirling and teasing, building the tension until she's quivering right on the edge. With a final swipe of my tongue she shatters, her body convulsing, her cries of pleasure echoing around us in the truck bed.

I continue to lick and suck, drawing out her orgasm until she's limp and breathless. I lift my head, my gaze meeting hers, the satisfaction of seeing her so thoroughly spent filling me with pride and contentment.

"*Oh my god*, Griff," she whispers, her voice hoarse with emotion. "That was...amazing."

I smile. "That's just the beginning, Pixie Pie. There's so much more I want to do to you."

She grips my shirt as she pulls me closer. "Show me, Griff. Show me everything."

CHAPTER 4
STEVIE

R eally? Griff has been in love with me this whole time? Just like I have been with him?

It's a crazy, beautiful miracle.

"Griff," I whisper, my voice hoarse, "I want you to fuck me. I need to feel you inside me." The words are both exhilarating and terrifying.

Griff's eyes widen slightly, a flicker of concern passing over his features. "Stevie, I'd love to, believe me. But I don't have any protection with me. I didn't exactly think—"

I run my fingers through his beard, soft and rough at the same time. "It's okay. I'm on the pill and have been for years." I bite my lip. "Just to keep my periods regular. I've...um... never actually been with anyone before."

"What?" He does an actual double take, then shakes his head as if he heard me wrong. "But...you...you're so sexy, so confident, so...*everything*?"

I laugh lightly. "It just never happened." I shrug, lowering my eyelashes. "And there may have been someone who was taking up space in my heart."

"Wow." He strokes a hand down my shoulder. "Well, I guess I have a confession to make too." He inhales deeply. "It's never happened for me either."

I blink rapidly. "Seriously? But everything you just…" I put a hand to my chest. "Griff, you blew my mind."

He beams. "I'm glad. But…yeah. Never wanted anyone else but you."

Holy shit, my heart…

"I'm nervous, Pixie Pie. What if I'm not good enough? What if I can't make it good for you?"

I lean in, pressing a soft kiss to his lips, feeling the warmth of his breath mingle with mine. "Teddy Bear, if it's anything like what you just did to me, you have less than zero to worry about. Besides, just being with you is more than I ever hoped for."

His arms pull me tighter against him. "You are a dream come true, sweet girl. I'm still expecting to wake up any second," he murmurs.

"I'm as real as it gets, Griff," I say, pulling up his shirt.

He pulls it the rest of the way off as I run my hands over his chest, my fingers tracing the lines of his muscles, the softness of his belly. The contrast between his smooth skin and coarse body hair under my touch is electrifying. His breath hitches as I trail my fingers down to the waistband of his jeans, his thick erection straining against the fabric. I claw my nails over it.

"*Fuck…*" he breathes, shifting to help me unbutton his fly, finally exposing his massive length. I wrap my hand around it, feeling his heat and pulsing desire.

"Shit, Griff, you've got a monster there."

His deep, primal groans fill the truck, sending a surge of passion through me. I stroke him gently, gazing into his eyes.

"This okay?" I ask.

"*Okay*?" He grits his teeth. "It's fucking magnificent."

He shifts to pull his jeans and boxers the rest of the way off, then his hands go right back to roaming over my body. He kisses me, his tongue swirling with mine, and when I taste myself on him, it sparks my senses. He trails more kisses down my neck, his hands cupping my breasts, thumbs brushing over my nipples. I arch into his touch, a soft moan escaping me as he works me over.

I reach down to touch him again and he shivers.

"You keep touching me like that and I'm going to blow, Pixie Pie."

I still my hand. "Well, when you put it that way..." I say, guiding his cock to my pussy.

"You ready?" he asks, his voice low.

"More than ready," I reply.

He growls as he presses a soft kiss to my lips before slowly pushing into me. There's stretching and pressure, and a slight pinch, but it eventually gives way to a deep, overwhelming pleasure.

Griff is inside me.

He whispers curses. "You feel incredible, Stevie. So hot and wet and perfect."

"I swear I can feel you everywhere. Even up in my throat," I say.

He chuckles, but when he starts to thrust, making me whimper, he pauses and kisses my cheek. "We'll ease into it, baby."

As he moves, it's admittedly a little rough at first. But my muscles slowly relax enough for me to wrap my legs around his waist, pulling him deeper, feeling the connection between us growing stronger.

"Damn..." Griff moans, his strokes firm and deliberate, his

body in tune with mine. The rhythm builds, our breaths coming in short gasps, the heat and passion between us filling the air.

My moans get louder, each roll of his hips sending waves of pleasure crashing over me. The intensity ratchets higher and higher and I cling to him, my nails digging into the muscles of his back.

The tension builds, reaching a fever pitch, and Griff's movement becomes more urgent and erratic. His groans fill the truck. The friction, the heat, his sounds—it all pushes me over the edge, and I cry out. My orgasm crashes over me like a tidal wave, leaving me breathless and quivering.

"Oh god, Stevie..." Griff follows, his release accompanied by a deep groan and a final, powerful jerk. I can feel him pulsing inside me, filling me with his hot seed.

We collapse together, our bodies entwined, our hearts pounding in unison. Griff's arms wrap around me, pulling me closer. His body provides me with a wonderful sense of security and comfort. I love it.

"Spectacular," I rasp.

"Pretty sure I left my body for a moment there," he mutters.

I chuckle. "I'm glad you came back."

"Me too." Griff smiles and kisses the top of my head.

I snuggle into his embrace as the events of the day replay in my mind. The intimacy we've shared, the love that has blossomed between us, this moment, this entire night...they're all something I'll cherish forever.

As we lie together, the moonlight filters through the windows of the truck, illuminating our faces. Everything feels *right*. We're safe, we're together, and we've found a transcendent love.

"We're in trouble, aren't we?" Griff says.

"We sure are."

Because going back to how we were before is impossible now.

CHAPTER 5
GRIFF

The sunlight streaking into the truck and the soft touch of Stevie's fingers over my body stir me from the depths of a deep sleep. I had been dreaming of my purple-haired pixie, our laughter, our lovemaking, and our children as we grew old together.

It was like a fairy tale come to life.

My eyes blink open to see her tracing patterns on my chest, my belly, circling my navel. The gentle drag of her nails makes my stomach muscles quiver, and I squirm.

"Somebody's awake," she whispers in a devilish tone, propped up on one elbow, her gaze locked onto mine. A smirk plays over the corners of her mouth. "Morning, sleepyhead," she says, her fingers now sliding down to my cock, which jumps to attention under her touch.

"Morning, Pixie Pie," I moan. "Wow. You sure know how to get a man…up."

"I couldn't resist. You're just so sexy, Teddy Bear." Her fingers continue their exploration, tracing every sensitive vein and ridge, her touch sending jolts of pleasure to each lucky nerve ending.

She leans down, pressing soft kisses to my torso and my thighs, her lips trailing a path of fire. "I love your body, Griff. Every part of it." Each word is punctuated by a kiss that feels almost reverent.

"It's not too much?" I ask.

She shakes her head. "Not even close."

I watch in awe as she takes her time, her fingers and lips worshiping every single inch of me. I still can't believe this woman is here with me, touching me like this.

She drops a line of kisses down to my groin, her breath hot on my sensitive skin. When she takes my rock-hard length in her mouth, a loud groan tears from the depths of my soul with a rush of ecstasy and urgency that has me clenching the blankets beneath me.

"Goddamn, Stevie…"

She sucks and licks, her tongue leaving me utterly at her mercy. Her soft murmurs vibrate against my skin, adding more layers of pleasure. It's like she knows exactly what I need, what I crave, and she's determined to give it to me.

I'm lost in a fog of sensation, my body responding to her every touch and stroke. She works me over with a skill that has my hips grinding, seeking more of everything. Her hands roam over me, her nails digging into my skin as if staking her claim on my body.

I'm breathless, my heart pounding. This is more than just physical; it's an emotional and mental bond that is growing stronger with every intimate touch. It's a slice of heaven, a sense of completeness and fulfilment that I've never known before.

Stevie's pace increases, her mouth and hands moving in sync to bring me to the edge of the cliff. My body arches against hers as my release approaches.

When it hits, I'm helpless to do anything but roar. The force of my orgasm sends my body jerking and convulsing, and I grip the blankets tight.

As I come down from the high, Stevie gulps tentatively, freezing for a moment. *Wow.* She finally lifts her head, her eyes meeting mine.

"You didn't have to…swallow," I say, my voice husky.

"I know. But I wanted to," she replies, licking her lips.

Fuck me. "I'm… There are no words."

She rests her head on my chest. "I'm glad you liked it," she murmurs sweetly.

We kiss and it leads to more touching, more caressing. I find her tender little pussy and stroke it until she climaxes in my arms, and again we bask in what feels like a series of perfect moments all strung together.

Eventually, reality begins to seep in. "We should probably get going," Stevie mumbles.

I nod, kissing her hand. "I don't ever want to leave this truck. But yeah, you're right."

We reluctantly pull ourselves out of the warmth of the truck bed, the cool morning air a bit of a shock after the heated cocoon we've created. Stevie slips into her clothes and I do the same, my gaze lingering on her as she gets dressed. There's already an ache in my chest, knowing we're heading back to the real world.

The morning air is bright and fresh as we head to the gas station, walking side by side, the Montana landscape unfolding before us as I roll the busted tire along. We don't talk much. I think we're afraid to burst this bubble of joy. We stop to steal a kiss every so often as the sun shines down over the dew-kissed grass and towering pines that surround the road. It's a beautiful morning, one that we both want to savor.

At the station, the hum of machinery brings us back just a

little more to reality. Inside, the guy behind the counter with long, dark hair and a lip ring immediately zeroes in on Stevie.

"Hey there," he says with a smile, a predatory gleam in his eyes that sets my teeth on edge.

"Morning," I say, sharply, yanking his attention to me. "I have a tire that needs a fix. You guys do that here, yeah?"

The man nods, his gaze lingering on Stevie a little too long. "Of course. Anything else?"

Stevie opens her mouth to respond, but I cut her off, wrapping an arm around her shoulders possessively. "Nope, that's it."

Stevie slips her arm around my waist. "Thank you," she says cheerfully, dropping her hand down to squeeze my ass.

I jump slightly and grin at her.

He looks at us and shakes his head. "Right. Let me get that tire into the garage for you, and I'll ring you up."

As he moves away, Stevie turns to me, a soft smile on her lips. "I'm going to go wash up, Teddy Bear. Back in a minute."

I continue to keep watch over the guy, since he can't seem to take his eyes off my girl. It's not just jealousy; it's about ensuring that no one else gets too close to what's mine to protect. Yes, dammit, *mine*. I don't care what anyone says. Not even Harris.

"It'll just be a few minutes," the guy says when he returns from the garage. "That'll be 30 bucks."

I nod and hand him my credit card.

"That girl's a real babe," he continues, and I hold my breath, daring him to say something that'll require a fist to his jaw. "You're a lucky man," he says, and I relax.

"Don't I know it," I admit, blowing out a breath.

And as Stevie and I head back to my truck with our patched-up tire, I realize I don't know how I'm ever going to be able to pretend she's *not* mine when we get to the campsite.

CHAPTER 6
STEVIE

After Griff changes the tire, we get back on the road to head to Glacier Rim. Fortunately, our text last night to Harris and Finley to let them know what happened went through, and we're able to keep them up to date with our progress this morning as well.

Honestly, though? I lowkey wish we were still stranded.

When we finally pull up to the campground, my heart is racing. Harris and Finley wave excitedly, their smiles wide. But all I can feel is tension radiating from Griff, his hand clammy as he holds mine low beneath the dash, out of sight. This should be a happy moment, a time to announce the love we've found. Instead, it feels like we're walking into a minefield.

I give Griff a pointed look and he nods, letting go of my hand. I step out as Finley rushes over to pull me into a bear hug, her chestnut hair flying behind her. "You made it!" she exclaims. Harris follows, his eyes shining with a warmth that makes the knot in my stomach twist. "Hey there, sis." His deep voice rumbles as he wraps me in his beefy arms and kisses my temple. "You guys had us worried."

"Sorry, man, all my fault," Griff admits after hugging Finley, as Harris goes around to him. "I forgot to check the spare."

"It happens, buddy," Harris says, clapping Griff on the back. "As long as you kept this girl safe, it's all good." He smiles at me.

"Of course, he did," Finley chimes in. "Griff can be a super fierce teddy bear when he needs to be." She grins.

I force a nervous chuckle, glancing over to Griff. He's already unloading our gear from the truck. I catch his eye across the truck bed, and the longing in his gaze is like a punch to the gut. We're so close, yet so far.

I hate this pretending.

The rest of the day passes in a blur of forced cheerfulness. We set up our tents, gather firewood, and prepare dinner. Every stolen glance, every hidden touch, feels like a secret burned into my skin. The tension grows with each passing hour, the weight of it pressing down on me like a physical force.

As the sun goes down and the air gets chilly, we all gather around the crackling fire. We eat our smoked brats and coleslaw, then make sure to pack the food scraps and garbage into a special container and lock it in the truck. We don't need any real bears added to this mess.

Before we start making the s'mores we relax under the stars. Harris and Finley sit on one side of the fire, their bodies pressed close together, their faces lit up by the dancing flames. Griff and I sit across from them, our knees touching every so often as we recline in our camping chairs, bathed in the soft orange-yellow glow.

I watch Harris laughing and joking with Finley, his arm wrapped protectively around her shoulders. Dammit. That should be me and Griffin, too. The resentment builds like a firestorm in my chest, threatening to consume me. Finally, I can't take it anymore.

"I have something to say!" I exclaim, standing up and staring at Harris.

His brow furrows, but he raises his arms. "Then say it, sis!" he replies jovially.

I swallow, eyes darting from Harris to Finley to Griff, whose concerned expression makes me pause, but only for a moment. Fuck it. I can't keep it inside anymore.

"I'm in love with Griff," I say, spitting the words out before I lose my nerve.

Nothing but silence follows, the flickering flames turning everyone's faces around the fire into angry red devil masks.

Harris and Finley stare at me. Are they shocked? Angry? Finley's mouth opens and closes like a fish, her eyes wide and unblinking. Harris's jaw clenches, his eyes boring into mine with an intensity that makes me tremble.

But then I feel Griff step up beside me, his hand slipping into mine. He stares back at Harris. "And I'm in love with Stevie," he says, his voice steady and unwavering.

Harris explodes, his face turning even redder, his fists clenching at his sides. "You son of a *bitch*," he roars, rushing toward Griff. Griff doesn't back down, his stance wide, his shoulders squared. Harris shoves him, hard, and Griff lets go of my hand to keep his balance.

"I've always tried to think of her only as a sister, Harris. For the sake of my friendship with you. But my feelings are too strong. I can't deny them any longer."

Finley looks back and forth between us. "Harris," she says, her voice pleading. "You need to back off. They're both adults. If they want to be together, you can't stop them."

"Hell *yes* I can," Harris snaps, then turns to her, eyes blazing. "This is between me and Griff, Fin. Stay out of it."

"*Excuse me*?" Finley's jaw sets, and she jumps up, hands on her hips. "No, it's between you, Griff, Stevie, and me. We're all family here, Harris. You can't just ignore their feelings because you think you know what's best for your sister."

Harris rubs his hands over his face, his shoulders sagging. "I just don't want her to get hurt."

Griff steps forward, his voice softening. "Harris, I would never do anything to hurt her. You *know* me. I love her more than I can say."

Harris looks at him, his eyes reflecting the flickering flames. "But what happens if it doesn't work out? What happens if my best friend and my sister end up hating each other because they break up? What then, Griff?"

Griff's eyes never leave Harris's face. "Then we deal with it. Together. But you have to trust me on this one. You have to believe that I love her enough to do right by her. When have I ever done anything to make you doubt me?"

Harris doesn't respond, his jaw still clenched. The tension between us all is suffocating.

Griff finally breaks the silence with a sigh, turning to walk away. I watch him disappear into the darkness, my heart breaking more with every step he takes away from me.

Finley reaches out, her hand gripping mine. "Stevie, I'm so sorry. I had no idea..."

I shake my head, tears stinging my eyes. "It's not your fault, Finley. You didn't know. I should have told you both sooner, but I didn't realize Griff felt the same way about me until last night."

Harris covers his ears and shakes his head, bellowing, then storms off in the other direction.

"Boys," Finley grumbles, throwing her hands up in exasperation. I chuckle in spite of my fragile state. Then she pulls me into her arms. "Stevie, you really feel this way about Griff?"

I nod. "I know I don't have any experience with relationships. But I do love him more than anything, and I have for a long time. I can't think of anything but being with him—forever."

Finley smiles, her eyes shining with warmth. "Then you should fight for him, girl. Love like that is always worth fighting for. Harris will come around." She pushes a strand of hair from my face. "Go find your pig-headed brother. If he won't talk to you, tell him to come see *me*."

She smiles and I snort, giving her a squeeze. "Thanks, bestie."

I take a deep breath and walk away from the campfire, the warmth of the flames fading behind me as I step into the darkness.

A few hundred yards away, I find Harris sitting on a boulder by the edge of the campsite, his head in his hands. He looks up as I approach, his gray eyes sad in the moonlight. "Stevie," he says, his voice hoarse with emotion. "I'm sorry."

My defenses crumble. I sit down next to him, and put a hand on his broad back. "What can I say, Harris? I love him. We want to be together. We want to have a future. And, I mean, we could do that even if you didn't support us...but I'd much prefer that you were on our side."

Harris groans. "Watching our parents split up damn near killed me and sent me running from everything. I just hate to think that could happen to you. I don't want you to risk ending up alone and broken."

I shake my head. "Me? Broken? Sometimes I think you don't know me at all."

He freezes as if taken aback, then his eyes go soft. "Maybe I don't. I missed a lot while I was gone. I regret that."

"I regret it, too. Those ten years you were working in Alaska after Mom and Dad split really hurt, having you so far away while I was growing up." I watch his eyes carefully. "Never mind me: I'm not sure you know Griff either. Because he'd never hurt me. He would do anything to protect me." I huff, trying to lighten the mood. "Much like you, ya big ass."

He chuckles and blows out a breath. "You're right. I just need time to accept the fact that my little sister is growing up and making her own choices. About love. With—*ugh!*—with my best friend."

I smile. "That's all I ask."

Harris stands, giving me a hand up that pulls me tight against him. "I love you, Stevie. Always will. No matter what happens."

I hug him back. "Same. Always."

Then he flings me over his shoulder. "Hey!" I screech, as he starts walking.

Back at the campsite, I hear Finley groan as we approach. "Put her down, you big bully."

My brother sets me on the ground more gently than I expect.

"You okay now, Mr. Growly?" she asks Harris sternly, her hands on her hips.

He grabs Finley, cupping her face, and kisses her lips possessively. She looks almost drunk when he finally pulls away. "I'm so sorry, Finley. I deserve to be punished later for talking to you that way earlier."

"Gross!" I stick a finger down my throat and make a gagging sound. "Please stop!"

Finley nervously adjusts her clothes. "Sorry, Stevie. He forgets who's around sometimes." She glares at him. "Everything *else* okay now?"

Harris nods, a small smile on his lips. "Yeah, we talked. It might take a little time, but I'm willing to make an effort. For Stevie. For Griff. For *all* of us."

Finley smiles at him, her eyes shining with love. "I knew you would. But there's someone else you need to apologize to." She takes Harris's hand. "And a panty-melting kiss won't work on him."

Harris grimaces and I chuckle along with Finley.

CHAPTER 7
GRIFF

I stomp through the underbrush, the crunching of leaves beneath my boots matching the angry rhythm of my heart. The cool night air does nothing to soothe the rage burning inside me.

I honestly thought I was doing the right thing, confessing my love for Stevie, but now I'm not so sure. The pain in my chest only grows with each step away from the campsite and away from her.

The deepening darkness out here among the trees mirrors the worsening chaos inside me. I remember back when Harris and I were inseparable: the laughter we shared, the adventures we had. But all I can feel now is the sting of betrayal. I never wanted to come between him and his sister, but it seems like I've done just that.

I find a secluded tree stump wide enough for me to sit on. Memories of me and Harris flood back—late nights riding our bikes, ice cream at his dad's store, sneaking beers around the campfire when we got a little older. Harris was always there for me, as I was for him. But now everything feels broken, our friendship crushed to pieces like the dead leaves beneath my feet.

The sound of snapping twigs has me on alert. It's either a moose, a bear, or Harris—and I don't know which I'd rather face right now.

I turn and Harris walks up, his face a storm of emotions. Then his shoulders slump and he stuffs his hands in his pockets. "I've been a total prick," he mutters. "All because I'm a big dumb scaredy cat. But my insecurities and mistakes shouldn't be your problem."

I can see genuine fear and concern in his eyes. The pain in them cuts deep, and my anger starts to dissipate.

Harris rubs his hands over his face. "I've hurt her so much already," he whispers. "I wasn't there when she was growing up..."

I stand up and put a hand on his bulky shoulder. "But you're making it up to her every day now. She knows that." I kick the dirt. "We want the same things for her, you know. To make her happy. To keep her safe."

"If you love her, and she loves you, then... That's all that matters." Harris finally smiles. "But you'll need to be patient with me. Okay?"

Relief floods through me, and the tightness in my chest loosens. "Harris, I'm going to marry her. You're going to have so many nieces and nephews, you're not going to know what to do with yourself."

Harris's eyes widen, and then a smile spreads slowly across his face. "That would be the best gift, Griff. Family." He pulls me into a tight embrace.

I clap him on the back, our shared laughter filling the night air. Our friendship feels renewed and strengthened by our honesty.

Harris shakes his head, his hair flowing around him. "We

talked about this when we were younger, remember? The families we'd have, the places we'd live. I have to say, I never thought it would be *quite* like this, but here we are."

I nod, thinking back to those childhood dreams. "Here we are, indeed. I swear, having Stevie as my wife and you as my best friend is a dream come true."

Harris grins, his eyes shining with unshed tears. "I'm proud to call you my best friend, Griff, and I'll be even prouder to call you my brother when the time comes."

The weight of those words settles over me like a comforting blanket, and I feel a profound sense of belonging. We hug once more, and make our way back to the campsite.

Later that night, in our tent, Stevie and I are coming down from yet another round of truly sublime orgasms. We kept as quiet as we could, which was damn hot in and of itself.

Now she lies on top of me, as I stroke her back.

"Pixie Pie?"

Mmm-hmmm?" she murmurs sleepily.

"Marry me."

Her head pops up. "Did you just—"

"I did indeed."

She muffles a squeal and nods, kissing me feverishly.

"I think I need a verbal yes," I chuckle, holding her close.

"Yes, yes, *yes!*" she whispers, punctuating each word with a kiss. "I love you, Griff."

I squeeze her against me. "And I love you too, Stevie."

Her head falls back to my chest.

"You know, we should hold off on telling Harris for a bit," I add. "He knows it was my intention to ask you to marry me, but I don't think he thought it would be by the end of this trip. Besides, I need time to buy you a ring."

She chuckles. "Good call." She shifts to lie beside me, her leg casually slung over my groin. "You know I don't care about a ring. I just want to be with you."

"I know." I trail a finger over her thigh. "But I *want* to get you something to wear that reminds you of me always."

"How about a tattoo? I have the perfect one in mind."

"Yeah?"

She tilts her head to look up at me. "Yeah. A teddy bear. Right here." She points dreamily to the top of her left ring finger.

I groan. "Does that mean I have to get a tattoo of a...pie?"

"Oh, brother." She digs her nails into my side, and I stifle a laugh.

Then my future wife kisses me and I thank my lucky stars for the millionth time.

EPILOGUE - GRIFF

ONE YEAR LATER

The bell over the door tinkles and I look up from behind the counter to see my beautiful wife waddling into the general store. Her belly is enormous, stretching the fabric of her sweater to the limit, but she's an absolute vision.

I rush to her side, my hand gently taking her elbow. "Pixie Pie, what are you doing here? I asked you to tell me when you go out, for your own safety." I've told her again and again that now that she's so close to her due date, she needs to let me know where she is in case she goes into labor.

She smiles up at me, her eyes sparkling, and I instantly forgive her for everything. "I just needed to get out of the house and pick up some books from the library," she says, her hand gently resting on her belly.

"And that's fine, but text me next time. Please."

"Okay, Teddy Bear," she agrees, and I lean down to give her a kiss.

I swat her luscious ass and lead her to a chair near the counter, making sure she's comfortable before getting back to work.

The store is buzzing with activity, the familiar sights and

sounds already a part of my soul. The scents of polished wood and fresh produce mingle in the air, and the hum of conversation from customers drifts around the space. I've changed quite a few things in the store since I took over but made sure to keep everything that made it special to the community, including the Nolan name. It was my way of showing respect to my new family. Since the day I took over from my father-in-law, the shop has become my second home, a place where I can build a future with the woman I love. And while I might miss being one of Deepwood Mountain's mailmen, my new career as a shop owner is everything I dreamed it would be and more. Also, I still get to see Stevie as often as I want, given that her salon is just down the street.

"Did you check in with Mathias today?" I ask, handing her a bottle of water. She promoted Mathias to salon manager and he's been instrumental in keeping the place humming along while Stevie's been taking a step back. No way was I going to let her spend all day on her feet working while she was pregnant.

"I did. He said the new stylists are doing great. Not only are they ready to take over my clients while I'm on maternity leave, they can start building their own client base too. I'm thrilled!"

"That's a relief," I reply. I know she's been worried about her clients. But it seems everything will work out just fine. My chest swells with pride. "I'm so proud of you, Stevie. You're really building something special with that place."

She grins. "Thanks, Griff. I couldn't have done it without your support."

I press a soft kiss to her forehead. "Oh, I bet you could have," I say, winking. "But you're welcome anyway."

Our baby is due in a month, and I'm so ready. I've got my father-in-law, sister-in-law, *and* my best friend on call in case we need help. The store is running smoothly, and everything is set for the little one's arrival. I can't wait to meet our child, to hold them in my arms for the first time.

"Oh my god, Harris is texting me *again*," Stevie says, pulling her buzzing phone from her bag. "No matter how many times I tell him I feel like a whale, he still keeps asking how I feel," she grumbles.

I waggle my eyebrows. "He cares about you, that's all. For the record, you're the sexiest damn whale I've ever seen."

She just rolls her eyes.

Back at home, we settle on the couch in our cozy living room, and I wrap my arms around Stevie, pulling her close. "I'm so grateful for everything we have, Pixie Pie. Our family, our friends, our businesses. It's all just...perfect."

She smiles up at me, her eyes shining with love. "It really is, isn't it? We're blessed, Griff. Truly blessed."

I run my hands through her hair and relax to the sounds of the crackling wood in our fireplace.

"Oh! I forgot to tell you earlier," she says, grabbing at my shirt. "There's a new guy over at the Deepwood Library. His name's Hawk. He works with their computer systems. Eden introduced me." She shrugs. "He's kinda cute."

I narrow my eyes. "*Hawk*? What kind of name is that?" I growl, jealousy churning in my belly.

She drags her fingers through my beard, forcing me to look at her. There's a smile on her face that tells me she knows exactly what to say to get a rise out of me. Over the past year, she's made it clear she quite likes my possessive side. Probably because it always tends to lead to me claiming her sweet little pussy up against our front door, in the backseat of the truck, or on the checkout counter of the store after closing time.

Just to, you know, name the first places that spring to mind.

I slide my hand into her panties and find her pussy slick and ready for me already. "Judging by how wet you are, Pixie Pie, I think I need to show you again who you belong to."

She nods. "Definitely. I need *constant* reminders. Pregnancy brain and all that."

I grin. "Get up. I want you on all fours, baby."

And as the fire flickers beside us, I take my wife from behind, until we both come hard and collapse in a sweaty, satisfied heap.

"You do know I'm just teasing right?" she whispers as we lie there, letting our breathing return to normal. "I mean, I've had to endure quite a bit of your teasing since the first day I met you."

"Oh, I don't mind the payback." I roll over and nuzzle her neck. "Now, let's hear it. Who do you belong to, Pixie Pie?"

"To you, Teddy Bear," she says, and kisses my palm. "Only you."

"That's right," I reply. "Only me. Forever."

Want to read more from Husky Valley?
Check out the **Husky Valley** series page:
https://www.lexihayes.com/series/husky-valley

Need to catch up with the main Deepwood Mountain books?
Check out the **Deepwood Mountain** series page:
https://www.lexihayes.com/series/deepwood-mountain

You can sign up for my newsletter via my website:
www.lexihayes.com

It's the best way to hear about new and upcoming releases, plus get access to subscriber exclusives and bonus content.

And as always, if you liked this story, please post a review on any of your preferred platforms. Reviews are the lifeblood of independent authors like me, and I welcome your opinions and feedback.

Thanks for reading!

CATFISHED BY THE IT GUY

CHAPTER 1
EDEN

Bleuuurrrgghhhh.

My usual late afternoon slump hits me, the rows of shelves and computer workstations all blurring together. The thud of returned books coming down the chute, the chirp of the scanner, and the precise thump of my due date stamp blend into a soothing rhythm as I stand at the circulation desk. I sigh, rubbing my eyes as I glance around the Deepwood Library. Don't get me wrong: I *love* my job and the satisfied feeling that comes with helping the community. It's a comforting routine and one that I'm thankful for. Plus, if you love the smell of books, it's a little slice of heaven. But lately, it feels like something's...missing. Like I'm stuck reading the same paragraph while the rest of the world keeps turning the page.

Mrs. Martin, one of our oldest patrons, shuffles up to the desk with a pile of books in the basket of her walker. She slides them onto the counter. Nothing but romance novels, every time. I don't blame her. I love them, too. But the woman has read everything, and I mean, *everything*. From reverse harem to monster to BDSM. Even the ones that make *me* blush.

I must've made a face because she winks at me. "You know, dear, I've read so many of these books over the years that it would make your head spin, and I can tell you one thing—the *real* hero is never the one you expect."

I laugh lightly as I scan the books for her. "I'll keep that in mind, Mrs. Martin."

Great. I'm such a lost cause the 80-year-olds have taken to giving me advice.

As she slowly makes her way to the door, I glance at the clock. Almost closing time, and that means another night alone in my apartment, endlessly scrolling dating apps, hoping to find that elusive man of my dreams. I've kissed more frogs than I care to remember (um, and maybe done more than kissed a few of them), always ending up with the same gaping hole in my heart. I know the busybodies in town talk, but *I am not easy*. I'm just…willing to put myself out there. And dammit, the clock is ticking. I just turned thirty, for god's sake! My sister and my friends, all younger than me, are *married*! To rugged Adonises, no less. It's frustrating as hell.

Why can't *I* find my Mr. Right?

My phone buzzes in my pocket, and my heart leaps as I slip it out.

There it is—my one glimmer of hope that the right man for me is out there.

It's a notification from the dating app I signed up for three nights ago.

Someone calling themselves "Humble🩶Throb" has sent me another message.

I look around, feeling a flush creep up my cheeks, and then dash into my office. The door clicks shut behind me, and I lean against it, heart pounding as I tap on the notification.

Humble❤Throb: *I can't help it, StorytimeSiren, you've been on my mind all day.*

I keep picturing us together, curled up on the couch, your head on my chest as you tell me all about your day at the library.

But of course I'd have the hardest time keeping my hands to myself. Because my god, I'd love to trace every single curve of your sweet body, learning the secrets behind every gasp and moan.

Does hearing that make your heart race the way it does mine?

Did you think about me today?

Tell me you feel this strange and wonderful connection between us, too. Tell me I'm not alone in this craziness.

Oh. My.

I literally fan myself with my hand, heat pooling in my belly. This guy sure does have a way with words. Apparently, he's new to Deepwood Mountain, a day trader who works from home. He says he's looking for all the same things I am— a deep, real connection, a love that will last, a partner to share quiet nights and big dreams with. And judging by his photo, he's hot too—like, *scorching* hot. Dark hair, chiseled jaw, eyes that I swear are staring straight into my soul. It's not just his looks, though; it's the way he writes. He seems to understand me like no other man ever has.

Emphasis on *seems*. Is it too good to be true? With me, men have a habit of saying one thing and meaning the complete opposite. I've been down this road so many times, and it always leads to a dead end. Am I nuts for thinking this time it could be different?

There's a soft knock at the door, and Willa pokes her head in. "Eden? Everything okay? I saw you dash in here like your panties were on fire."

Oh girl, you have no idea.

I open the door wider, attempting to hide my flustered state. "I'm fine. Just... checking something."

She raises an eyebrow, a teasing smile on her lips. "Some*thing*, or some*one*?" She walks in and shuts the door behind her, sitting on the edge of my desk. She crosses her arms, settling in for the interrogation. "Okay. Spill."

I sit down in my chair and laugh nervously. "Oh, you don't want me to talk your ear off about some guy I'm chatting with online."

She leans over and places a hand on my arm. "Eden, I have a child at home who would rather eat paste than the meals I make her, who asks the same question over and over until I want to tear my hair out, and who lies about nearly everything. The only chance I get to be alone with Dash these days is for five minutes after the kiddo has gone to bed. But we're both so exhausted from our days we end up falling asleep before we can even *do* anything. Now, you're going to tell me about this new guy because I need some excitement in my life over and above the thrill I get from seeing a completely empty book return cart."

I blink, holding back a small smile. "His name is Humble Heartthrob. It's really cute, he spells it with a heart emoji. He's on Heart Sync, that new dating app, and he is...something else. Check it out." I hand her my phone, the message still open on the screen.

She scans it, her eyes widening. "Wow, Eden. This dude is...intense." She taps his profile and uses two fingers to make his photo bigger. "Shit, girl! He's a major hunk."

"I know, right?" I take the phone back, clutching it to my chest like a smitten schoolgirl. "He's smart, funny, he's traveled all over the world. And he says he wants to settle down, that he's looking for something long-term."

Willa looks at me, her expression serious. "That's really awesome, Eden. But…"

"How do I know he's not a big, fat fake?"

She bites her lip and makes a face. "Well…"

"I *don't* know. And I won't know until we meet." I shrug. "That's just the way it is with online dating."

She nods. "Well, promise me you'll be careful. You've been hurt a few times, and I'd hate to see that happen again."

I lean back in my chair. "Tell me about it. I've been burned more times than a scented candle in a powder room. But Willa, he just…he gets me. You know how hard it is to find someone who actually sees me for me, and not how the town gossips paint me?"

Willa squeezes my hand. "I do. And I really want you to find that perfect someone. Just make sure he's worthy of you, okay? Don't let your heart run away with your head."

Willa's so sensible. She has a way of keeping me grounded, and I love her for that. "You're right. I need to do some detective work. Make sure he's not just another toad in prince's clothing."

Willa grins, standing up. "Fantastic! So, how are you going to do that? Background check? Secret stakeout?"

I glance through the glass wall of my office just as Hawk Tate, the library's new IT director, walks by with a stack of books. He's cute in a nerdy sort of way, with his thin-rimmed round glasses, and slightly rumpled shirt. Not my kinda guy physically, but there's still something endearing about him.

And everyone says he's a *genius* with computers.

"I think I have an idea," I say, watching Hawk as he walks away down the hall. "The new IT guy Hawk—he's brilliant with tech stuff, right? Maybe he can help me track down Humble Heartthrob, make sure he's not a scammer."

Willa's eyes light up. "That's a great idea! You really should get to know him better anyway. He's so shy, and since he's new to Deepwood, I'm sure he'd be happy to have more friends. Who knows, he might make you forget all about Humble Heartthrob. Maybe what you're looking for is hiding in plain sight behind glasses and a keyboard."

I roll my eyes, laughing. "Please, Willa. You know me better than that. Hawk may be sweet and all, but he's a bit younger than me, and not...well, he's not the kind of guy I usually go for, you know what I'm saying?"

Willa shrugs. "Okay. I tried. I guess I just want you to remember you have options. *Someday your prince will come...*" She starts to sing as she gets up from my desk and twirls around.

"Okay, someone's gone a bit loopy," I say, shaking my head. "I am definitely no Snow White. I think it's time Auntie Eden took the little one off your hands for a couple of days, Willa."

She blinks at me, her lower lip trembling. "Really?"

"You name the weekend and I'll be ready."

Suddenly, she flings herself into my arms. "Thank you, thank you, *thank you!*"

I'm laughing as I hug her back.

She pulls back. "You're the best, Eden. I mean it."

"Question: How much chocolate is too much chocolate to give her?" I ask.

She plugs her ears. "La la la la...I am not listening..."

She hustles out of my office.

A buzz of excitement runs through me. Time to find out if my online admirer is really the man of my dreams, or just another Kermit.

CHAPTER 2
HAWK

Tucked away in my office, servers humming and monitors glowing, I stare into the computer screen, willing the code to fall into line as my fingers fly over the keyboard troubleshooting some back end issues with our eBook checkout system.

"Validate, dammit!" The cursor just blinks, taunting me. "Why you suboptimal, bug-ridden piece of—"

Ping.

A notification that I've received a direct message on the library's chat system pops up.

From *Eden.*

My heart leaps into my throat, as it always does when I see her name. I haven't even read the message yet, but my palms are sweating. I push up my glasses, taking a deep breath before clicking on it.

> Can you meet me in the foreign translations section at 1pm? I have a favor to ask.

I gape at the message, my mind racing.

What could she possibly need from *me*? I'm just the IT guy.

There's no *way* she could've found out I'm Humble Heart-throb. Right? I mean, I've been so careful.

No one pays any attention to me back here in my little cubbyhole of an office. Not like I mind. I'm much more comfortable with machines and code than people, preferring the clicks of my mouse to the quiet chatter of library patrons.

God, why did I have to send off that note during work hours? Because I got greedy, that's why. I needed to tell her how I feel. How she drives me crazy. I couldn't help myself.

The woman is everything I'm not—extroverted, confident…sexy. She knows exactly what she wants and goes for it, end of story. She's not afraid to put herself out there and take risks. I envy that.

I've always been too introverted, too shy, too…I'll say it… husky. I've never been the kind of guy women like Eden go for. Yet here I am, drawn to her like a node to a network.

I hate the fact that she keeps going for the wrong guys— who don't see her for who she truly is and don't treat her with the love and respect she deserves.

I glance at the clock. It's almost 1. I should make my way to our meeting spot, but I'm rooted to my chair, my heart pounding in my chest. I'm playing with fire. I've been walking this tightrope for too long, juggling my online persona and my real life. The guilt gnaws at me, but it's outranked by the thrill of our online connection.

I force myself to stand, running a hand through my hair distractedly. I really like it in Deepwood Mountain, and the library, and…Eden. I honestly could see making a life here and would hate to ruin everything.

That's it. I'm going to stop sending her messages on the

dating app. No more Humble Heartthrob. Yes, she'll think he's a jerk who lost interest, but it's the right thing to do. I can't keep deceiving her.

I check my breath to make sure it doesn't smell like stale coffee (all good there), then tuck my shirt in a little better before heading toward the foreign translations section. I can't help but notice the way my shirt pulls slightly at my midsection. I've always found solace in food and in the comfort it brings. But suddenly, I'm hyper aware of my soft gut and wish I was more like the men Eden usually goes for— athletic, with a six pack.

When I arrive Eden is already there, her back to me, fingers tracing the spines of the books. She's wearing one of her brightly colored vintage dresses that accentuates her hourglass figure, her rich, dark hair pinned up on the sides, the rest falling to her shoulders in a casual retro style.

She's an angelic vision. Effortlessly stunning.

She turns as I approach, her smile lighting up the dim corner. My heart skips a beat and warmth spreads across my cheeks. Oh god, please don't let her notice.

"Thanks for meeting me," she says, her voice barely above a whisper. She reaches out and grabs my hand, pulling me in closer. Her eyes dart around anxiously until she's satisfied we're alone, then she grins up at me. It's the closest I've ever been to her. The tall shelves loom over us, forcing me to inhale her sweet perfume—a spicy, floral scent that tickles my nose. I try not to notice the way her eyes are studying me, traveling over my cheeks, then lower to my lips. It's almost as if she's never seen me before. She's probably rethinking whatever "favor" she wants to ask me. But her hand is still holding mine. I itch to stroke my thumb over her soft skin.

"No problem," I manage to say, my voice surprisingly

steady. She lets go of my hand and I hastily shove them both into my pockets, trying to look casual. I lean against the shelf, and a couple of books promptly fall out. Smooth.

"Shit," I curse under my breath, leaning down to pick them up. "Sorry."

"It's okay," she chuckles. "I'll put them back in a sec. I'm good at that."

I nod, setting the books on top of a nearby stool.

She takes a deep breath, her cheeks flushing slightly. "So, um...I met this guy on a dating app. He goes by Humble Heartthrob. With a heart emoji, not the word."

Oh god. I'm so busted.

Why am I like this? Why can't I just ask a woman out like any other normal man on the planet?

Her gaze drops. "He's smart, funny, really sexy and..." She trails off, her eyes flickering back to mine.

Here it comes.

"I like him, but I need to know if he's for real. And I thought maybe you could help me with that."

My heart hammers in my chest.

Wait, what?

This is my chance to man up and tell her the truth. Like, right on a platter in front of me.

But the words die in my throat when I see the hope in her eyes. "Eden," I start, picking my words carefully. "It's not always easy to track these guys down. They use fake names, fake photos—"

Her face falls, and I hate myself for putting that disappointment there. "But," I add hastily, "I'll do whatever I can to help."

You're an idiot, Hawk. A big, cowardly, stinking idiot.

She smiles again and my world spins in a happy circle. "You will? You have no idea what this means to me! His messages... They make me feel like there's someone out there who understands me, you know? Someone that I really *mean* something to. Thank you so much, Hawk."

And just like that, I'm sucked back in. How can Humble Heartthrob ghost her now? I can't, not when she looks at me like that. Like I'm her hero. Now that I know what my messages do to her, I'm in too deep.

"So, what exactly do you want me to do?" I ask, trying to keep my tone professional.

She bites her lip, thinking. "I don't know. Are you able to trace his profile? Find out who he really is?"

I laugh, running a hand through my hair. "It's not quite that simple. These apps have privacy policies, encryption. It's not like in the movies where you can just hack into the mainframe."

She pouts, sticking out that luscious lower lip and giving me a sudden wave of dizziness. "Crap. Okay. Then what can you do?"

I grab the bookshelf to steady myself. Then she crosses her arms, her breasts pushing upward. *Initiate emergency protocol!* I swallow and clear my throat. "I can try running an image search, see if his photo pops up anywhere else on the internet. I can also try to find out more with the info you have. There are ways to cross-reference information, see if it matches up."

Her eyes widen. "Wow, you really do know your stuff."

I shrug, looking down at my feet. "It's just what I do. I'm better with data than people. Data follows rules, has patterns. People, they're a crapshoot."

"I think you might be selling yourself short, but...yeah, I get it." She rubs her pretty hands together, a gleam in her eye. "Okay, when can we start our investigation?"

"Whenever you like. I'm at your mercy." I huff. "I mean, *service*."

Get it together, Hawk.

She grins. "How about tonight? You can come over to my apartment. I'll make you dinner to thank you for your help."

My heart pounds in my chest and the dizziness threatens to come back. Dinner? At her place?

Shit, that's…nerve-wracking. But wow, it's also a chance to spend more time with her. To get to know her better. To show her that I'm more than just "the IT guy".

"That sounds great," I say, trying to keep my voice from cracking. "What time should I come over?"

She thinks for a moment. "How about 7pm?"

I nod. "It's a date."

The words pop out before I can stop myself. I freeze, my eyes widening in horror. "I mean—not a date. Just… dinner. And work. Investigation work."

Eden laughs, her eyes sparkling. "All good, Hawk. I knew what you meant."

I breathe a sigh of relief, chuckling nervously. "Good. I wouldn't want you to get the wrong idea. I'm just the IT guy."

She looks at me, her expression serious as she eyes my mouth. "Hawk. You're *not* just the IT guy."

I gulp. "I'm…I'm not?"

She taps my chest with her long nails, and I nearly gasp from the sudden contact. "You're the IT *Director*. Remember that."

I deflate like a sad balloon.

Yeah, well, you walked right into that one, dummy.

"'See you tonight, Hawk. I'll send you my address," she says, and turns to walk away, her dress swishing back and forth. Soon I'm alone in the foreign translations section, my mind spinning.

I take a deep breath, trying to calm down. Tonight is my chance. My golden opportunity to prove to Eden that I'm a good man who is worthy of her time. But how am I going to do that while simultaneously pretending to track down the man of her dreams?

Fuck.

I'm so going to blow this.

CHAPTER 3
EDEN

The knock at my door is dead on time. I would expect nothing less from Hawk.

When I open it, though, I'm caught off guard. The man on my porch is...*kinda hot*. He's swapped his unofficial work uniform of button-down shirt and dress pants for a fitted forest green Henley and dark jeans that hug his thick thighs. His hair is slightly tousled, the green of the shirt bringing out not only the red highlights in his hair, but the same mossy shade in his hazel eyes.

He's actually a really big guy, tall and broad, with a strength that's more apparent now that he's not hunched behind a desk. And he carries his weight well. It's a good look.

"Hi," he says, offering a small smile as he holds out a bottle of wine. "I don't know anything about wine, but I figured red was a safe bet?" When I don't respond right away he hurriedly adds, "I know this isn't a date but my mom taught me always to bring something when you're invited to anyone's house and I had no idea what else I should bring and—"

"This is perfect." I interrupt his flood of words with a

chuckle, stepping aside to let him in. "Come on in, make yourself comfortable."

As he walks past me, I catch a whiff of his cologne—something woodsy and earthy with a hint of sweetness. Maybe vanilla? Whatever it is, it makes me want to lean in closer to see how it smells on his skin.

Nope. Won't be doing that. Nope, nope, nope.

I take the wine from him, our fingers brushing briefly, and a spark of electricity shoots up my arm. *What's that about?* I shake it off and turn toward the kitchen. "This way. I made tapas. I hope you're okay with seafood. Everyone says you shouldn't have red wine with seafood but I say life's too short not to bend the rules."

Hawk follows me, his eyes scanning the array of dishes set out on the counter. "Wow, Eden. You made all this? It looks and smells incredible. I love seafood."

I beam at him, handing him a plate. "Then you'll love the *gambas al ajillo*. Help yourself. I'll just pour the wine."

We fill our plates and settle onto the stools at the kitchen island, and I tell him all about the dishes, watching as he tastes my food and gushes over every bite. Sitting with him here, outside of work, has me seeing him in a whole new light. The gentle way he handles the food, the appreciative noises he makes, it's all incredibly…oh dear…sexy.

I take a sip of wine—*Spanish, so he gets bonus points*—and serve him another helping of *arroz al horno*. "Okay, you have to tell me how you ended up with the name Hawk."

He looks up at me, a soft blush spreading across his cheeks. "I know. Most guys called Hawk ride big ass motorcycles and make pilgrimages to desert caves to find their spirit animal. Cool shit. I'm not cool."

I chuckle. "Um, I don't think I said that."

"Didn't have to. Most people are thinking it," he says with a shrug. "But the thing is, my name isn't actually Hawk. Hawk is short for Hawking."

I raise an eyebrow. "Hawking? As in Stephen Hawking?"

He nods, a small smile on his lips. "Yeah. My parents are both scientists. My dad's a professor of physics at the University of Montana, and Mom is an astronomer. They were both obsessed with Stephen Hawking, so..."

"Wow, that's amazing," I smile. "It suits you. You're brilliant, just like him."

Hawk's blush deepens and he ducks his head. "Oh, I wouldn't go that far. But thank you."

I nudge his foot with mine under the island. "Well, you're one of the smartest people *I* know, at least."

He looks up at me, his eyes meeting mine, and there's a moment of charged silence between us. *Why am I feeling like this? Did I seriously just play footsie with the guy?* No matter what Hawk might be outside of work, he's still Hawk Tate, IT Director of Deepwood Mountain Library, here to help me figure out if the man of my dreams on the other side of my internet connection is actually who he says he is. I nod toward his laptop. "Should we start?"

Hawk licks his lips, then wipes his hands and mouth on a napkin, pulling his laptop closer. "Sure. Let's start with the photo. I'll run a reverse image search and see what pops up."

As he types away, I watch as his fingers dance over the keyboard with practiced ease. Never rough or sloppy or heavy handed, just gentle and insistent. I wonder if that's how he'd be handling *me*—

Eden!!!

"Eden," he says, drawing my attention back to the screen. "I hate to say this, but Humble Heartthrob's photo is a fake. It's a stock image."

126

Oh.

I try not to get too upset as I lean in to look at the search results. "Damn. But that doesn't for sure mean he's a catfish, right? Maybe he just didn't feel comfortable putting his real face out there?"

Hawk nods, though I can see concern in his eyes. "Yeah, it's not totally conclusive. Let's see what else we can find."

As he continues his search, I refill our wine glasses and bring out more food. He has another serving of *patatas bravas*, his eyes rolling back in his head as he groans happily. "God, Eden. You're a fantastic cook, you know that?"

I smile, feeling a warmth spread through my chest that has nothing to do with the wine. "Thanks. Cooking is my family's love language, I guess. My sister and I learned from my mama, just as she learned from hers."

He looks at me, his eyes shining. "Well, she taught you well. Honestly, I could eat this every day."

He takes another bite, and a big blob of sauce drips onto his shirt. He looks down and curses. "Wow. Slick, Hawk."

I giggle and jump up to snag a clean dishcloth from the linens drawer, plus some seltzer water from the fridge. "Here, let me help."

I sit down next to him and reach out to dab at the stain, but Hawk grabs the napkin from me, slight panic in his eyes. "It's okay. I got it."

He just smears it.

He looks down at his shirt, then back up at me with an embarrassed sigh. "Okay. You win. I need help."

He hands me the cloth, and I gently dab at the stain with a clean corner of it. As I do so, I notice the way his shirt stretches across his chest, and how his breath maybe hitches whenever I touch him. I can feel the heat of him and the strength of his muscles beneath the fabric. Yet despite his size, there's a certain softness to him that's borderline irresistible.

Watch it, Eden.

I finish cleaning the stain and step back. "It's going to need some time to dry, but it should be fine now."

"Thanks," he says, then turns back to his laptop. "Obviously, we don't have a name, but maybe it has Humble or Heart in it?"

I grin. "Like Bret Hart the wrestler?"

He laughs. "Exactly. Though I hate to disappoint you, it's probably not him. Let's see if we can find any property records on the local assessor's site with either of those names."

As he types away, I lean in, watching as he pulls up different websites and enters various search queries. Damn. He really knows what he's doing.

"Anything?" I ask.

He shakes his head. "No. Can I see one of the messages he's sent from the app?"

I bite my lip. "Do you have to? It's, um, kinda personal."

He smiles. "I'm not going to read it. I'm just going to look at the code behind it to see where it's coming from."

"Well, if you must," I say doubtfully, and pull it up on my phone.

He taps a few things, then hands it back to me.

"That's it? So fast."

"Yep, I sent the code to my laptop. Now I'll run it through some sites."

"Wow," I scoot a little closer to him, watching him work. "You're amazing."

"Got it!" He pulls up a map. "I found the IP address linked to his account. It's here in Deepwood Mountain."

"Really? So, whoever is using that account really does live in Deepwood Mountain? That's good news, right?" I squint at the map. The IP address comes from a street I've never heard of on the edge of the mountain. "That's pretty remote," I say, a mix of excitement and nerves churning in my stomach. "I feel I should go see if it looks legit. Will you come with me?"

Hawk swallows nervously, his eyes darting to mine. "Eden, are you so sure that's really a good idea?"

I wave a hand dismissively. "Oh, come on. It's not like we're going to knock on his door and demand answers. We'll just drive by and see what kind of vibe we get."

Hawk hesitates. "What if it's a twelve-year-old kid?"

I roll my eyes. "Trust me, a twelve-year-old kid does not write like this."

"What about a sixty-year-old serial killer who makes skin suits out of his victims?"

I do a spit take with my wine, then playfully smack his arm. "*Hawk*! You can't be serious."

"Why not?" he chuckles. "It happens."

I reach out, placing a hand coaxingly on his arm. "How about this? I ask Humble Heartthrob out on a date. If he shows, we won't have to go to his house."

He looks down at my hand, then back up at me. Then he gulps. "Okay," he says, a resigned sigh escaping his lips.

"Thank you, Hawk."

He blushes. Oh my *god* it's adorable.

We finish our meal and I pack up the leftovers. I hand them to him as he prepares to leave. "For you. To say thanks again for tonight." Then I press up on my tiptoes to kiss his cheek before lowering myself down again.

He inhales quickly, his eyes riveted on my lips.

I bet they're stained like his from the wine. I wonder what they'd taste like now.

Hawk moves away and takes the container. "Thanks, Eden. Glad I could help."

I walk him to the door. "Goodnight," he says, his voice soft.

"Goodnight, Hawk," I reply. "See you tomorrow."

He waves as I close the door behind him. A longing, a desire for something real, something true, blooms in my belly. And as I lean back against the door, I wonder if Humble Heart-throb is really the one to give it to me.

CHAPTER 4
HAWK

I step into my apartment, the chill of the Montana evening trailing behind me, so different from the warmth I felt with Eden. My heart is still pounding from the day's and then evening's events, each beat echoing her name. I flick on the lights, my home feeling suddenly emptier than usual.

I set the bag of leftovers on the counter, the aroma of our shared meal filling the kitchen. I put the containers in the fridge, remembering how her eyes lit up when I complimented her on her cooking. How impressed she appeared by my online research skills. She even called me brilliant! Every moment with her feels like a treasure to be carefully stored away and cherished.

As I close the fridge door, I catch myself grinning like an idiot, a giddy sensation bubbling up inside me. I'm falling for her. *Hard*. It's not just the crush I had before. It's something deeper, something that's growing. She's not just the gorgeous librarian I fantasized about from my dark cave of an office; she's sweet, witty, and kind. She's everything I've ever wanted in a woman. More.

I should be ecstatic, but there's a gnawing unease in the pit of my stomach. I'm leading her on, both as Hawk and as Humble Heartthrob. I'm the one she's confessing her desires to, the one she's sharing her intimate thoughts with, but from behind a veil of deceit. I'm helping her investigate a man who doesn't exist, all the while knowing that I'm the guy she's looking for.

It hurts my brain trying to sort it all out.

I lean against the counter, my reflection in the glass of the cabinet staring back at me accusingly. What the hell am I doing? Setting myself up for heartache, that's what—worse, I'm setting Eden up for disappointment. She deserves better than this. She deserves honesty, sincerity, and truth—all things I'm completely failing to give her.

I should come clean, but I can't. I'm a coward, too afraid to risk losing her, even if it means keeping on deceiving her.

My phone buzzes in my pocket, and I pull it out to check the notification. It's Eden, messaging me on the app. Well, messaging Humble Heartthrob.

Oh god.

As I settle on the couch, sinking back into the cushions, I make a silent promise. I'll make this right. Somehow, some-way, I'll find the courage to tell her the truth. But not tonight. Tonight, I just want to lose myself in our conversation, pushing aside my guilt and letting myself be swept up in the whirl-wind that is this amazing woman.

> **StorytimeSiren:** *You're* not *alone, Humble* 🤍 *Throb. I do feel it—this wild connection, I mean. I think it's safe to say we're both a little crazy, right? I couldn't stop thinking about you at work today. How could I after such a sweet, sexy message? You have an incredible way with words, and I'm hooked on them.*

Heat spreads across my cheeks as I quickly but carefully type my response.

Humble💜*Throb: You don't know what that means to me, hearing you say that. I'm addicted to your messages, too. And knowing you feel the same way makes my heart want to burst.*

StorytimeSiren: I do have a confession to make, though. I'm curious about you, and I did a little digging. That profile photo…it's not you, is it?

I take a deep breath, only pausing for a second.

Humble💜*Throb: You caught me. That photo isn't me. I'm sorry. I wasn't sure how to approach someone as beautiful as you. I was worried I wouldn't be attractive enough for you. Your beauty is… intimidating.*

Her reply comes swiftly, and I can almost hear her smile through the screen.

StorytimeSiren: Attractive enough? Sweetheart, I'm sure you're a dream. Why don't you let me *be the judge of that?*

Sweetheart. I like that. I see my opportunity and grab it with both hands.

Humble💜*Throb: Let's meet, then. Just say the word and I'm there.*

Her message bubble appears and disappears a few times as she composes and edits her reply. I hold my breath.

StorytimeSiren: You read my mind. How about tomorrow night? Marge's Diner at 7:30pm? I can't wait to see the man who's been filling my head and making me blush at odd moments throughout the day.

I quickly tap out my response.

Humble💙*Throb: I'll be there. But I'll be nervous. You promise to go easy on me?*

StorytimeSiren: Cross my heart.

We continue to chat, and before I know it, we're getting into deeper, sexier territory. Eden's words are like a spark, igniting a fire within me. It's insane.

StorytimeSiren: Are you in bed yet?

I get up from the couch and walk over to my bedroom, falling back onto my bed.

Humble💙*Throb: I am now...*

StorytimeSiren: Me too. And I can't stop thinking about what you'd do to me if you were here right now. Can you tell me?

My breath catches and I groan, shifting on the mattress. Does she really want to go there? My cock is already hard and pulsing in my jeans. I know I shouldn't, but I can't say no, even if she does think I'm someone else.

Humble💙*Throb: You really want me to tell you? I don't want to scare you off if I get too...graphic.*

StorytimeSiren: You won't scare me off. It actually kind of turns me on thinking you might be too much for me to handle. 🔪 *LOL*

I choke out a laugh and begin typing out a response, my fingers hovering over the keys as I imagine her here next to me.

Humble💜*Throb: I'd run my hands through your hair, tilting your head back so I could gaze into your beautiful eyes. Then I'd lean in and kiss you slowly and deeply until you were breathless.*

Her reply comes quickly.

StorytimeSiren: And I'd slide my hands over your broad back... and then lower, pulling you up against me. Would I feel how hard you are?

Humble💜*Throb: Fuck yes. I'd be as hard as a steel beam. Are you touching yourself right now?*

StorytimeSiren: I've taken off my pajama top and I'm stroking my breasts.

Holy shit. A groan escapes my lips, and I can't resist any longer. I unbutton my jeans, sliding my hand into my boxers, feeling the heat of my arousal. Every nerve ending is alive with fiery excitement.

Humble💜*Throb: That's so hot, baby. I'd let my hands wander down your exquisite body, committing every sweet sound you make to memory. I'd cup those perfect breasts, teasing your nipples until they were hard and aching for more.*

StorytimeSiren: I love a teasing touch. You're making me so wet. I wish you could see me right now, see what you do to me.

The image of her, flushed and aroused, sends a jolt of desire through me. I stroke myself, my grip tightening as I imagine her body writhing beneath me.

Humble💜*Throb:* I'd trail kisses down your neck and your collarbone until I reached your breasts. I'd take one into my mouth, licking and sucking until you were crying out for more.

StorytimeSiren: God, I'm reaching into my panties and teasing my wet pussy just thinking about that. Arching my back as you work my nipples. I wish it was your hand in my panties and not mine.

Humble💜*Throb:* Me too, baby. I'd kiss every inch of your skin, making my way down to that dripping wet heat between your legs. I'd taste you and lick you and suck your clit until you couldn't take it anymore.

StorytimeSiren: Yes, yes, lick me…fuck, that's soooo good. I'm so close. I can feel it building. I want your cock inside me. I want you to fill me up and take me completely.

A growl tears from the back of my throat and my breath comes in ragged gasps, my hand pumping my cock faster as I read her words.

Humble💜*Throb:* I'd slide into you, slow and deep, feeling every inch of your pussy gripping me.

StorytimeSiren: God, yes! I'm sliding my fingers into me, imagining it's you and your thick, hard cock. Fuck, you feel amazing.

Christ, I'm close, so close, my body tense, aching for release. My mind is filled with images of her, her body arching, her luscious lips parted as she cries out my name.

Humble ♡ Throb: I'd thrust into you again and again, rolling my hips to find every spot that makes you scream my name over and over. I'd claim you. You'd be mine, completely and utterly mine. I'm going to come, baby…

StorytimeSiren: Oh, fuck yes. I'm yours. All yours. I'm cominnnnng! Coming so hardddd.

Her words push me over the edge, and I come too, my body shuddering its release. I let out a low groan, my heart hammering in my chest as I ride the wave of pleasure. The screen of my phone is a blur, but I can still sense the connection between us.

I manage to type with one finger as I lie there with my jeans open.

Humble ♡ Throb: Wow…I'm…that was…just WOW. You are incredible. Man, I need a towel.

StorytimeSiren: Ditto…to all that.

Humble ♡ Throb: What a way to end the night.

StorytimeSiren: If you thought I was hungry to meet you before, now I'm…ravenous.

Humble ♡ Throb: Ravenous. I like that. Tomorrow can't come soon enough.

StorytimeSiren: My thoughts exactly. Goodnight, sexy.

Humble💙Throb: Goodnight, baby. Sweet dreams.

I close the app and set my phone down, my heart still racing. I'm elated, but the feeling is tempered by a growing unease.

The lines between Humble Heartthrob and Hawk Tate are blurring. Eden's words, her flirtation, her confessions—they're all for a man she thinks she knows, a man that *I've* created. But the feelings she stirs up within me are painfully real.

I want her to look at *me* the way she does when she reads Humble Heartthrob's messages, with a spark in her eyes and a smile playing on her lips.

The thoughts keep me awake long into the night. I struggle with the truth, trying to find a way to untangle the web I've spun. But every option leads back to the same place: telling her. Somehow, I have to find the courage to reveal the truth and hope that the connection we've forged is strong enough to withstand my deception.

CHAPTER 5
EDEN

The library is unusually quiet as I make my way to the foreign translations section. Willa is off today, volunteering as a parent chaperone on her daughter's school field trip. Horrible timing, considering I have *so much* to tell her.

I sent a note to Hawk asking him to meet me "in our usual spot" so I could at least tell *him* the news.

When I round the corner, I see Hawk already there, leaning against the shelf, reading a book. Something about him looks different today, but I'm not exactly sure what. He's wearing his usual office attire—loose button-down shirt and khakis—but today the sleeves are rolled up, revealing muscled forearms. His glasses are perched on his nose with an air of authority, and his hair is a little deliberately mussed up. It's…sexy. And when he glances up as I approach there's a spark in his eyes that hits me low in my belly.

"Hey, Eden," he says, his voice deeper than I remember, as he closes the book and shelves it.

I lean in, getting closer than I probably should. "Hey, Hawk."

He smiles down at me. "Thanks again for that amazing

dinner last night. I can't wait to have the leftovers for lunch today."

"You're very welcome," I reply, putting a hand on his bicep. It flexes.

Damn, that's…firm.

I take my hand away, clearing my throat. "Humble Heart-throb beat me to the punch asking me out."

"Really? That's great," he says. "When?"

"Tonight. 7:30 at Marge's Diner." I shrug. "So, you're off the hook going with me to scope out his house."

He huffs playfully. "Well, I'd be lying if I said I wasn't relieved."

I try to ignore the sudden flip in my stomach when I hear Hawk's husky chuckle.

"We did have a good time last night though, right?" I grin. "For someone so shy, you're actually pretty fun. Maybe we could do it again sometime."

I'm remembering how easy he was to talk to, how he made me laugh. It was…nice. More than nice, if I'm being honest.

He's blushing now. And damn, it really is adorable. "Sure. I had a great time last night, too."

Hawk clears his throat, looking slightly flustered. "Well, if you need anything tonight…you know, if things don't go as planned or he's a creep or whatever…you can always call or text me."

I smile, grateful for the offer. "Okay, will do." We pull out our phones and exchange numbers. "Thanks."

"Good luck tonight," he says, his smile almost sad. "But do be careful. Please?"

"I promise," I reply, before he walks off, back to his office.

I'm left standing there staring after him, wondering why I'm suddenly so confused.

Guilt pokes at my insides. Maybe I shouldn't have sexted

with Humble Heartthrob last night. Even if I did imagine it was Hawk doing those dirty things to me...instead of my faceless online admirer.

Later that evening, I'm a huge bundle of nerves as I sit at Marge's Diner, waiting for Humble Heartthrob. I'm also wondering why we didn't bother to exchange real names.

Probably because that would make it more real.

But...that's what I want from him. Something real! Duh!

My stupid inner voice has been piping up at inopportune times ever since I left Hawk earlier today, and I don't know what it wants from me.

The truth, girl, that's what.

The *truth* is I want to meet the man behind this silly handle, because he makes me feel things. He's not like all the other men I've met. He's different. He's special.

Like Hawk...

What?

Don't play dumb with me, woman. I know you.

I shake my head, I don't have time for conversations with myself. Instead, I breathe in the comforting aroma of grilled food and baked desserts and listen to the buzz of friendly chit chat around the diner. But honestly, my attention is all on the door. It's just after 7:35 and he's still not here. I check my phone repeatedly, rereading our messages from last night. Everything felt so right—not just the sexting, but the conversation, the *connection*. I couldn't possibly be wrong about that, could I?

7:45.

As the minutes tick by and my soda glass begins to sweat onto the table, I realize he's not coming. I've been stood up. It's definitely not the first time in my dating career, but I really,

really thought this time would be different. A wave of disappointment washes over me, settling heavily in the pit of my stomach.

Before I can wallow too much, I pull out my phone and dial Hawk's number. He answers on the first ring.

"Eden? Everything okay?"

I take a deep breath, realizing how much I like hearing his deep voice. "He didn't show, Hawk," I mumble.

There's silence for a moment, then— "Be there in ten."

Hawk walks into the diner just as I'm finishing my soda. He's in jeans and a sweater and he looks dreamy. He slides into the booth across from me, concern etched all over his face.

"I'm so sorry," he says, and I swear, the way he apologizes, it's almost as if *he* was the one who stood me up.

I wave him off. "It'll be fine. But now, I've changed my mind. I'm having the pot roast with mashed potatoes and a hot fudge sundae for dessert. Screw the salad idea. Wanna join me?"

"Sounds good," he says, a smile spreading over his handsome face.

We order dinner, and despite the crappy start to the evening, I find myself enjoying myself thoroughly. The way Hawk tells jokes…listens to me…teases me but nicely…it all makes me feel seen in a way that I never thought I would.

We end up sharing the sundae. And of *course* that has me thinking of what else I could lick hot fudge sauce from. I know, I'm shameless.

When the night finally comes to an end, Hawk insists on paying and walks me to my car. The night air is cool, the stars twinkling above us. He leans down to open the car door for me, and I put a hand on his arm.

"Hawk, thank you for being there for me tonight. I had

such a good time despite the evening starting off on such a crappy note. You really saved me."

He smiles softly, his cheeks pink. "Anytime, Eden."

Before I can second guess myself, I lean in and press my lips to his. He still tastes like hot fudge topping. For a moment he freezes, and I worry I've made a huge mistake, but then his firm lips give way and he's kissing me back. His hands come up to cup my face gently and he groans as his thumbs stroke my cheeks. The kiss is soft, sweet, and...*wow*.

I pull back, slightly breathless. "Do you, um, want to come back to my place?"

Hawk looks at me, his hazel eyes filled with longing, but then he shakes his head. "I want to, Eden. You have no idea how badly." He glances down at his feet. "But I don't think it's a good idea. Not after what you've been through tonight."

I swallow, nodding. "I get it. You're probably right."

"Besides," he sighs, "I wouldn't just want this to be a fling or a one-night thing."

He opens the door and I get in, letting his words settle over me.

They sting.

Because he's right. You need to figure out what you really want before you make a mess of his emotions.

This time I listen to my inner voice.

As I drive home, it hits me that I'm more disappointed with Hawk turning me down than I was with Humble Heartthrob standing me up.

What's up with that?

CHAPTER 6
HAWK

The library is buzzing when I arrive, but today I couldn't care less.

I'm exhausted…and totally heartsick.

I guess that's what happens when the woman you're madly in love with asks you to come home with her—after a kiss that rocked you to your very core—and you turn her down.

God, I'd wanted to say yes. Wanted to make love to her all night long, exploring her sweet body. But I just couldn't. Not with the secret I'm keeping, and especially not when she'd just been rejected by a jerk from a dating app.

Yes, I *know* that jerk was me. But *she* doesn't.

I want Eden more than anything else in the world. But I want her to want me back, not just because some online admirer ghosted her, but because *I'm* the one she can't get enough of. The one she truly loves.

I spent all night thinking about her and the crushed look in her eyes when I told her I couldn't go back to her place. Well, maybe that was wishful thinking. Not that I *want* to disappoint her, of course. It's just…ugh, this is confusing…it would be nice to think she might've been a little heartbroken... over *me*.

Of course, she probably wants nothing to do with me or any other guy now anyway.

I don't see her all day, which I guess is for the best. I'm training our new support tech right now, and can't afford to be distracted. I bury myself in work, trying to ignore the gnawing, empty feeling in my chest.

As the day winds down, I'm finishing up some reports when my computer pings with a message from the library intranet. It's from Eden.

Meet me in our spot?

I fix myself up, chew a mint, and head toward the back of the library. When I turn the corner, my heart almost stops when I see her. Her dark hair is pinned back from her lovely face, a green button-down dress cinched at her waist and draping playfully over her mesmerizing hips. Her cleavage has me salivating.

She sees me and smiles, but it's a softer, more intimate smile than usual. "Hi," she says.

"Hi." I try to sound casual, but inside my heart is pounding. How close to her should I stand? How close would she *like* me to stand?

She grabs my wrist and pulls me closer, answering my question. She takes a deep breath. "About last night..."

I know she's going to tell me off. Call me an asshole for kicking her when she was already down, reeling from rejection.

She looks me straight in the eye. "I'm so sorry, Hawk. I've been stupid and inconsiderate." She inhales deeply. "I...uh... have feelings for you. *Strong* feelings."

What the—

To say I'm stunned is an understatement. I open my mouth to speak, but no words come out.

She places her palm on my chest. "You're sexy, Hawk. You really are. From your kind eyes to your big, rugged body. Plus, you're funny, and sweet, and wickedly smart. Seriously, you're one of the nicest guys I've ever met, and you've only ever treated me with respect and honesty."

A brief wave of guilt washes over me at her use of the word honesty, but it's quickly replaced by a flush of sheer exhilaration. Eden—the gorgeous, seductive librarian of my fantasies —has feelings for me? I can't believe it.

"But I do have another confession." She glances down at her hand on my chest, and I hold my breath. "Humble Heartthrob and I got pretty...um...hot and heavy online that night he asked me to meet up." She gulps. "We sexted." She throws her shoulders back and looks up at me with a sad but determined expression. "I shouldn't have done that when I was having these new feelings for you. I just...I don't know...got caught up in his words and the way you'd made me feel earlier. And...not that it makes it any better...but I imagined it was you the whole time."

I blink. Is she kidding? That makes it *a thousand times* better.

"I'll understand if that's a deal breaker, and I'm sorry, Hawk. I really am. If I could go back, I would never have done it."

"Eden, I—"

"There's more." She puts her fingers to my lips to silence me. God, I'm about to melt. "If you can forgive all that, I want to be with *you*, Hawk, and only you. We can take it slow if you like. Get to know each other better, taking it one day at a time."

Oh my god. I could burst—from everywhere. My heart is racing, I'm starting to sweat, and my cock is raging in my khakis.

"No," I blurt out, and her eyes widen, her mouth dropping open as she backs up.

"No?" She deflates right before my eyes, but I pull her hand back to my chest.

"I mean no, I don't want to go slow. I'm in love with you, Eden. I've been in love with you since the first day I met you. I just wanted you to want me the same way I do. I need you."

I grab her face and kiss her sexy mouth as she yelps, caught off guard. The kiss is not soft and sweet like last night's. It's fierce, passionate, and filled with all my longing. I can't hold back. I kiss her like I've been wanting to for weeks, my hands tangling in her hair, the pins falling out as I pull her closer to me.

We stumble back against the shelves, books and metal rattling around us. I'm consumed by her, by the taste of her, by the feel of her luscious body against mine.

She whimpers, clawing at me, nipping at my lips.

"Hawk," she moans, swiping her tongue deep into my mouth, writhing against my body.

Something primal takes over inside me, an intense surge of possessiveness as I lift her up and carry her to a nearby table.

I lay her down gently on the cool, smooth wood. My hands glide up her thighs, and her breath catches as I run my fingers along the hem of her dress. I push it up slowly, revealing more of her creamy skin, my heart pounding. I see the pulse in her neck quicken and watch her breasts heave. Her thighs part, inviting me in, and I trail my fingertips over them, feeling her shiver beneath me.

"Yes. Touch me," she says on a soft breath.

Leaning down, I press wet kisses along the insides of her

thighs, feeling her muscles contract under my lips. I move higher, kissing every inch of her skin like it's sacred ground. My own personal Valhalla.

Her hands spear through my hair, gripping tightly, urging me on.

"You're driving me wild, Hawk..." she cries. I love being able to tease her and savor her anticipation. I can feel her impatience, her pure need, in the way she squirms beneath me.

"Fuck, these panties are sexy," I growl, running my thumb along the wet fabric, pressing into the seam of her pussy.

"Oh *god*," she groans, and I can't wait any longer.

I pull up a chair in front of her and push her sweet thighs apart, shoving my nose against her drenched panties. Her intoxicating, sweet musky scent drives me crazy.

"I need to devour this hot, wet pussy," I rumble. She's panting as I pull the panties aside and slide my tongue along her molten flesh, feeling her shudder.

She's delicious.

She tastes like a warm, rich autumn day. I explore her with my tongue, learning what particular spots make her gasp and moan and pull my hair tighter in her fists. I circle her clit and her body jerks, her hips lifting to meet my mouth.

"*Goddammit*, Hawk," she whines, her body trembling.

She's so beautifully responsive, so alive under my mouth. I continue to feast on her sweetness, my cock throbbing in my pants, dying to have her lose control and fall apart beneath me.

I alternate between sucking on her clit and dragging my tongue over her velvety skin, moving in a circular rhythm that matches the pace of her ragged breaths. She's getting closer, I can feel it in the way her body is tensing up and her moans are growing louder. I don't stop. I don't slow down. I keep going, pushing her higher and higher.

Suddenly she comes with a cry, her body convulsing, her hands shaking in my hair.

Yes, my sweet…

I don't stop until her body relaxes and her breathing slows. Only then do I press one last kiss against her, looking up to meet her gaze. Her eyes are glassy, her cheeks flushed, and she's never looked more beautiful.

I did that. I made this sexy woman a panting pile of limbs on the library table. My heart swells with a mix of pride and awe. "You're a vision of loveliness," I murmur, my voice raspy.

A soft and languid smile plays on her lips. "And you, Hawk Tate, are a naughty, *naughty* boy," she teases, her voice breathless. I can't help but chuckle, feeling a wave of happiness that I've pleased her. I've dreamt of this moment over and over, but nothing could have prepared me for the reality of it.

A blush creeps up my cheeks. "I have a confession to make," I say, my voice barely above a whisper. "I…may have never done that before."

Her eyes widen and she grabs onto my arm. "Oral sex?"

I nod, feeling more than a bit self-conscious.

"Then you're a natural," she says, reaching up to cup my cheek. "And I'm honored and *so grateful* you wanted to do that to me."

I capture her hand, pressing a kiss to her palm. "The honor is *all* mine. Truly."

She wraps her arms around my neck, pulling me close. I can feel her heart beating against mine, and it's the most incredible feeling in the world. As she rests her head on my shoulder, her hands slide down my chest, tracing the planes of my muscles.

"I think *you* need some attention now," she whispers. She moves lower, her fingertips grazing the bare skin at the waistband of my pants. I inhale sharply, my body tensing.

She looks up at me, her eyes dark with desire, a wicked smile playing over her lips. "You want me to touch you, Hawk?" she asks, her voice husky and low.

"You never have to ask me that. I will always want your touch," I reply, my breath turning heavy as she slowly undoes my belt, then unzips my pants. She reaches inside, her fingers wrapping around my length, and I groan, the sensation of her touch on my cock overwhelming.

"That's some python you've got there," she says.

"Enough for you?"

"*More* than enough." She strokes me gently, her hand moving in a slow, torturous rhythm that makes my hips rock and buck against her.

"Eden," I gasp, holding onto the edge of the table for dear life. Her touch is electric, setting every nerve ending I have on fire.

She leans in, her breath hot in my ear. "You like that?" she murmurs, her hand moving faster, her grip tightening.

"Y-es..." I manage to choke out, barely able to form coherent words, my heart hammering in my chest.

She looks up at me, her eyes filled with a hunger that matches my own. "I want to taste you." I swallow hard. She moves off the table, her body sliding against mine, her hand still stroking me, driving me to delirium.

She sinks to her knees in front of me, her gaze holding mine. I watch transfixed as she leans in, her tongue flicking out to taste the tip of my cock.

"*Fuck...*" I let go of a shaky breath, the sight of her on her knees and the feel of her mouth on my cock almost too much to bear. She takes me deeper, her lips wrapping around me, her tongue working its magic.

All I can do is moan and tremble as I tangle my fingers

through her hair, guiding her. My hips move in rhythm with her mouth, her hand coming up to caress my balls.

God almighty...

Somehow, she manages to take me even deeper, her mouth hot and wet, her tongue swirling and tracing each contour of my throbbing cock.

My body coils with tension. "I'm close, Eden," I whisper, my voice hoarse.

Her hand comes up to stroke me in time with her mouth, and it completely scrambles my brain. She's working me over with such skill I can't hold back any longer. With a long, guttural groan, I come, my body shuddering as I spill into her mouth.

"Christ!"

She takes it all, sucking and stroking until I'm spent, my body limp and sated.

She places a single kiss on the tip of my cock before she tucks it back into my boxers. Then she sits next to me on the table.

"I can't move," I say weakly, and she giggles.

She lies down and traces the line of my jaw with her finger.

I wish I could lie here forever with her. But my needling conscience pokes me, disturbing my bliss. I know I have to come clean about Humble Heartthrob, about the lie that brought us together. But dear god, not now! Not while she's looking at me like this, her eyes filled with desire and affection.

Soon. Before it's too late. For now, I push the thought away, determined to just be present in this moment. That's enough. In fact, that's everything.

"Wanna come back to my place?" I ask, with a grin.

She bats her long lashes. "I thought you'd never ask."

CHAPTER 7
EDEN

The door to Hawk's apartment is barely closed behind us before he pulls me into his arms, his mouth finding mine in a hungry, fiery kiss.

I melt into him, my body aching with need.

I'm thrilled Hawk was able to see past my horrible lapse in judgment with Humble Heartthrob and give me a chance to show him how much I've fallen for him.

And to hear he's in love with me? That's the best news of all.

I jump into his arms and wrap my legs around his waist as he carries me into his bedroom.

"Eden," he whispers against my lips, before dropping me gently onto his bed. "I never imagined you'd ever be here with me."

I smile, nipping at his lower lip. "Well, I am," I reply, my hands sliding under his shirt to feel the warm expanse of his chest. He shivers at my touch, his eyes darkening.

He suddenly pulls aways. "A friend gave me a handful of condoms before I moved to Deepwood Mountain." He rummages in the nightstand next to the bed. "I guess he had a lot more confidence in me than I did."

He holds up a condom triumphantly and waggles his eyebrows.

I laugh as I sit on the edge of the bed and reach out to pull him closer by the belt loops of his khakis. I look up at him, enjoying the view of his thick, burly frame. "You're a little over-dressed, Hawk," I tease, my fingers working at his belt buckle.

He swallows hard, his hands trembling slightly as he helps me undress him. When his shirt comes off, it reveals a broad chest dusted with dark hair, and a sexy trail leading down into the waistband of his pants.

A thin silver chain with a strange rectangular pendant hangs around his neck. "What's this?" I ask, turning the plastic piece in my hand.

"It's a memory chip," he replies, with a weak smile. "All the members of my college coding club have them as a memento. We're called the Binary Bandits."

I press a hand over my mouth and chuckle.

"I know, I'm a total nerd." He shakes his head. "And that's probably not the best thing to tell the woman of my dreams right before we have sex."

"It's sweet," I say, but can't stop giggling. "I love it."

He chuckles along with me. But as I take in the expanse of his sexy bare torso, I press a kiss to his stomach, feeling his muscles quiver under my lips. He groans, his hands tangling in my hair.

I look up at him, a mischievous grin on my face. "I know you said you'd never gone down on a woman before, which I'm still having a hard time believing…" I trail off and bite my lip, recalling writhing under Hawk as he drove me out of my mind. "But how about the rest?"

His cheeks flush. "I'm not a virgin. But I've only ever been with one girl. Back at Cyber Summer Camp. It was…mostly just awkward, to be honest." He admits and shrugs. "Since then, I've been waiting for the right person, I guess."

I stand, wrapping my arms around his neck. "Well, I'm glad I get to be the right person," I murmur, before kissing him deeply.

He begins unbuttoning my dress, the feel of his fingers brushing over my cleavage giving me goosebumps. I unhook my belt over it and he pushes the dress down over my shoulders, letting it puddle at my feet.

He nuzzles his head between my breasts, then reaches around to unclasp my bra.

"Your breasts are perfect," he groans, cupping them and teasing the peaks with his fingers. "And so are these sexy hips and this juicy, juicy ass." His big hands slide down my body into the back of my panties and squeeze my cheeks.

He trails kisses down my neck as he fits me up against him, pressing his thick cock against my belly. Wow, the man really was blessed.

I help him out of his pants and boxers, and he's throbbing, the taut head dripping. I wrap my hand around him, and he moans low and deep, his body trembling.

"Eden," he whispers, his voice hoarse with need. "Show me how to fuck you the way you want."

I arch a brow. "Careful what you wish for."

He smirks, but then his eyes go wide when I push him down onto the bed. He flops onto his back with a heavy thud.

"Where's that condom?" I ask, peeling my panties off and tossing them aside.

He hands me the foil package and I crawl onto his thick body. Sitting up, I tear open the package with my teeth and roll the condom over his massive cock.

"And you said *I* was naughty," he chuckles, sliding his hand up my thigh.

I straddle him, lifting up on all fours. "You ready for me?"

"So ready," he breathes, and I guide his cock to my opening. I let gravity ease me down onto him, stretching me almost impossibly wide.

"Oh hell…" he huffs, tensing under me. He grunts as I take him deep inside me.

"You said it," I exhale, long and slow, nails digging into his chest as I adjust to his size.

"You okay, baby?" he asks, squeezing my flank.

"I'm great…just trying to let my body get used to you. I'm going to move now, okay?" I lean forward and start to roll my hips.

Both of us gasp.

"Wow," he says, his eyes closing. "That's really…*wow*."

His words encourage me to keep going, slow and steady, each movement bringing more pleasure despite how stretched I am. Soon we have a rhythm going, our bodies moving in sync, as we moan and whisper to each other.

His hands come up to palm my breasts, thumbs teasing my nipples, and my head falls back in ecstasy.

As I quicken the pace, he moves one hand down to my hips, adding more thrust.

"God, you feel so good." My climax begins to build, a spiral of pure need tightening in my core.

"Shit, baby, you're so fucking sexy. I'm not going to last much longer. That tight, wet pussy is making me forget my own name," he says between pants.

"I'm going to come, Hawk. I can't hold back either." I cling to him, my body arching as I spasm and shake, crying out his name.

"Fuck, yes!" He holds my hips tight against him as he

bucks up into me. "I'm there too, baby." His body shudders, and I feel the pulsing throb of his release. He convulses and jerks, then is still.

I collapse on top of him, my breath hot and ragged against his skin. I feel complete, whole. It's something I haven't felt. Ever.

"Love you, Eden," he says, stroking my back softly.

"Love you, too, Hawk," I reply.

I wake up to the warmth of Hawk's body next to mine, the events of last night rushing back into my mind like a vivid dream. The way he touched me...the passion in his eyes...the playfulness—it's more than I could ever have imagined. I slip out of bed and throw on my dress, leaving him to sleep, and tiptoe softly to the kitchen to make coffee.

As the coffee brews, I notice Hawk's computer set up on a desk next to the kitchen counter. I hear a familiar notification sound, and glance over at the screen.

*Humble💛Throb, you haven't talked to **StorytimeSiren** in over 24 hours.*

My world glitches and screeches to a halt.

Just then, Hawk walks in, rubbing his eyes sleepily. "Morning," he murmurs, then stops, seeing my expression. "Eden? Everything okay?"

I point at the computer. "Did someone put you up to this, or was this all your idea?" I whisper, the humiliation burning hot in my cheeks. "Pathetic Eden, desperate enough to fall for some guy on the internet and then jump into bed with the guy who just *happens* to be there when he lets her down? Using me? Laughing at me this whole time? Did you at least get what you wanted?"

"Eden, it's not like that—" he starts, but I can't listen. I'm too angry, too hurt. He said he *loved* me. How could he be so cruel to say that as a joke? Jeez, I bet the whole virgin thing was a lie, too.

"Save it, Hawk." I rush past him to grab my things, ignoring his pleas for me to stay.

"Eden, let me explain," he begs, as I get into my car.

"No. I'm done playing the fool." I slam the door shut and leave him standing there on the curb, his shoulders slumped.

I drive aimlessly, tears streaming down my face.

Why am I even crying over the dumb jerk?

Because you love him, silly.

Well, I'm an idiot.

Meh, maybe.

Nice, self. *Real* nice.

I pull into an empty park nestled into the base of the mountains and get out to sit on the hood of my car, letting the sun dry my face. The cool morning air is refreshing, but does little to soothe the fire raging inside me. My phone buzzes incessantly with calls and texts, presumably from Hawk, but I can't bring myself even to look at them.

Instead I call Willa and spill the entire sad story.

"Oh, honey," she sympathizes. "I'm so sorry."

"I've had my heart broken before, but this time..." I dissolve into tears again, and I can't help the sobs that tear from my throat. "It just hurts so bad."

"Eden, that's love. With all the guys in the past, I don't think you've ever been in love."

"But how could it have hit me so fast?" I whisper between gulping hiccups.

"I don't know, sweetie. Love is strange that way. It's never how you expect it to be."

I wipe my eyes with my skirt and take a deep breath, trying to get it together.

"You're probably not going to like what I have to say next…" she says, and I groan and let my head fall back to stare at the sky.

"What is it?"

"Maybe you should give him a chance to explain. Like, why would he go through all this just for a joke? You told me he said he loved you *after* he slept with you. Why would he let it play out that way if he was just using you for sex?"

"To have more sex in the future," I snap. "Like, duhh."

She chuckles. "So let's review. He's incredibly sweet, does nice things for you, tells you he loves you repeatedly, and you have great sex…potentially for weeks, months, years to come? Umm… Hate to break it to you, but that doesn't sound like a joke. That sounds like a relationship."

I blink. "It does?"

"Yeah. You've never been in one, Eden. How would you know?"

My mind reels. "I'm so confused."

Willa sighs. "It sounds like he just got caught making a few dumbass mistakes. We're all guilty of that, right?"

Ouch. I know she means some of my not-so-honorable actions in the past involving a certain Callahan ranch owner.

"Yeah, you're right," I groan. "I have to go back. I don't know how I'm going to face him without completely crumbling, though."

I can hear the smile in her voice. "This is amazing. I've never seen this side of you, Eden. Don't get me wrong, I hate that you're hurting. But it's refreshing to see you distraught over a man that might actually deserve you."

Her words stick with me as I drive back.

Hawk is sitting on my apartment steps when I pull up, his head in his hands. He looks as shitty as I do. Which makes my stomach do a strange flip flop.

As I approach, I see that his puffy, red eyes are filled with remorse. "I'll leave if you want me to, Eden," he says, standing up. "But please, just give me a chance to explain."

I nod and motion for him to follow me inside. I lean against my kitchen counter and cross my arms over my chest, trying to stay strong.

"Okay. Talk."

He takes a shaky breath, running a hand through his hair. "I—I was stupid to pretend to be someone else. But when I was Humble Heartthrob, I wasn't shy. I didn't stumble over my words. I could tell you exactly how I felt. And my god, you were so easy to talk to. You made me feel like I meant something." He grips the back of a bar stool, as if needing support. "I had planned to stop writing to you after those first three days, because it was starting to feel wrong, but then you asked for my help in checking him out, and it meant I got to spend time with you. That was a dream come true to be with you in real life. By that point, I was afraid you'd never talk to me again if I came clean."

I bite my lip to stop it from trembling.

"I wanted to tell you, Eden. I truly did. I just never could find the right time. Every moment with you my feelings kept growing. And as they did, so did the worry that I'd lose you." He gets down on his knees in front of me, sitting back on his haunches to look up into my eyes. "I'm begging you, Eden. Please forgive me. I'll spend the rest of my days making it up to you, I swear. I love you so much."

The pain in my heart begins to ease as I see him there, literally groveling. I lean down and run my fingers through

Hawk's hair. "Get up here, you," I say, pulling him up. He smiles down at me, and I feel a tear slip down my cheek. Hawk wipes it away with his thumb. "I'll forgive you, Hawk," I say softly. "If you'll forgive me. I think we've both made mistakes."

"You know I'd forgive you for anything." He strokes my jaw, and I nuzzle my face into his palm.

"I do love you, Hawk Tate," I say, then pull him down for a kiss. A long, deep, passionate one.

When we finally come up for air, I'm positively dizzy.

"I *knew* there was something special about Humble Heartthrob," I add, cuddling into Hawk's chest. "Besides his panty-melting sexting skills, of course."

His cheeks turn an adorable shade of pink. "How do they compare to my…in person skills?"

I chuckle and give him a wink. "Let's just say, I've officially just become the luckiest woman in Deepwood Mountain."

EPILOGUE - HAWK

ONE YEAR LATER

Eden and I step into Mama Alvarez's house, the aroma of fragrant spices and home cooking engulfing us. I bring in the various bags filled with the tapas Eden made earlier, packed into a cooler dangling from my arm. Eden's mama's house is always so full of life, with colorful plants everywhere, and I'm pleased to note that right now the tantalizing smell of *paella* is wafting through the air. Eden's *paella* is a close second, but there's something about Mama Alvarez's that's pure magic.

Of course, I'll go to my grave saying that Eden's is the best.

Mama Alvarez greets me with her usual warmth, pulling my face down to plant big smacking kisses on both cheeks. "*Mijo, bienvenido!*" she says, her eyes crinkling with joy. I can't help but smile back, her welcome as warm and comforting as the scent of her kitchen.

We make our way to the kitchen island, where Eden's younger sister Paige and her husband Reece are sharing a glass of wine. "Hawk!" Paige exclaims, her face lighting up as she comes over to give me a hug. Reece claps me on the back and gives me a firm handshake. "Great to see ya, man."

161

Eden rushes over, a whirlwind of energy, and hugs them both fiercely before diving in to help her mother. She's in her element here, cheeks flushed and eyes bright as she plates up the tapas we brought. I love watching her do this, her hands moving with surety and skill, just like when she's organizing books at the library.

Or when she's...*ahem*...never mind.

We've been inseparable since that day at her apartment. I've made it my mission to always show her how much I love her, and she's been nothing short of amazing. Her family has become my family, and Mama Alvarez never fails to tell me how much she loves me—although I think a lot of that has to do with how much I enjoy her cooking.

She does make a point to pull me aside frequently to whisper in my ear how happy Eden is these days, and it warms my heart to think I have something to do with that.

"Sorry we're late," Eden says, pouring us each a glass of wine. "We had to stop and help a woman lost on the road. She was looking for Radcliffe Farm, and you know how hard that is to find if you haven't been there before. Seems Zeke broke his leg and she's going to be helping him for a while."

"Whoa, I *do not* envy her," Paige says. "Zeke Radcliffe is a mean old coot."

"Paige!" Mama Alvarez swats at her with a dishtowel. "Where are your manners?"

"But she's right, Mama," Eden protests. "That man is grumpier than a mule with a burr under his saddle. I almost gave her the wrong directions because I felt sorry for her."

She and her sister giggle, but Mama Alvarez gives them a stern look that puts a stop to that.

"Watch it, ladies," she says, narrowing her eyes, pointing a serving spoon at the two of them menacingly. Then she breaks into laughter.

And the rest of us join in.

The conversation flows as freely as the wine as we eat, full of stories from Reece and Paige's animal sanctuary, the latest events from the library, and of course our upcoming trip to Hawaii.

That's where I plan to propose to Eden.

But as I listen to her sweet giggles and see the joy in her eyes as she interacts with her family, I realize I can't wait. This moment is so perfect, and I want to seize it. I reach into my back pocket and pull out the ring I've had for months now.

I get up and make my way over to her.

"What are you—" she says, but stops and claps a hand over her mouth, her dark eyes wide, when I get down on one knee.

Paige squeals as I take Eden's hand, and Mama Alvarez gasps.

"I love you, Eden. Ever since we've been together, you've made every one of my days brighter, every moment sweeter. I never want to be without you." I hold out the ring box and pop it open. "Will you please marry me?"

Tears well up in her eyes, but she's smiling and nodding. "Yes," she whispers, her voice thick with emotion. "Yes, Hawk, of course I'll marry you."

Reece lets out a cheer and puts two fingers in his mouth to whistle loudly. I laugh and slip the ring onto her finger before standing to pull her up and into a tight embrace. Mama Alvarez is crying happy tears, Paige is clapping, and Reece is grinning from ear to ear. It's perfect.

I'm surrounded by love and joy, and the most beautiful woman in the world has just agreed to spend the rest of her life with me.

Go figure. Catfishing the sexy librarian was the best worst mistake I ever made.

~

Want to read more from Husky Valley?
Check out the **Husky Valley** series page:
https://www.lexihayes.com/series/husky-valley

Need to catch up with the main Deepwood Mountain books?
Check out the **Deepwood Mountain** series page:
https://www.lexihayes.com/series/deepwood-mountain

You can sign up for my newsletter via my website:
www.lexihayes.com
It's the best way to hear about new and upcoming releases,
plus get access to subscriber exclusives and bonus content.

And as always, if you liked this story, please post a review on
any of your preferred platforms. Reviews are the lifeblood of
independent authors like me, and I welcome your opinions
and feedback.
Thanks for reading!

PLOWED BY THE FARMER

CHAPTER 1
DAISY

"It's *fine*. This is *fine*," I repeat to myself as I pull up to the old Radcliffe farm.

I feel like I've reached the edge of the world.

...and landed right in front of the farmhouse from *Night of the Living Dead*.

Clay had warned me the farm was "as far as you could go" on the outskirts of Deepwood Mountain. He wasn't kidding. It feels like I've been driving for ages since I left the main highway, constantly glancing in my rearview mirror expecting the monster from *Jeepers Creepers* to be following me.

I really shouldn't watch so many horror movies.

I'm just on edge because I'm out of my element. I'm not used to wide open spaces and large plots of land, or being so far away from the hustle and bustle of the city. I grew up with asphalt and high rises, not dirt roads and trees.

I take a better look at the acres of wheat fields, the golden stalks swaying gently in the breeze. I have to admit, it's picturesque...like something straight out of a painting.

Okay, maybe I didn't give the farmhouse enough of a chance. It *is* charming—more cottage-y than murder-y, with elaborate details on its white trim and a wide wrap-around porch. So...the 1990 remake of *Night of the Living Dead* rather than the 1968 original. Look it up if you don't know what I mean.

It's peaceful, the only sounds some sheep bleating in the distance and the wind blowing through leaves. Certainly a far cry from the honking of horns, pummeling of machinery, and loud chatter on the busy streets I'm used to. There's a sense of calm here, a tranquility that's pleasant, especially after the turbulent weeks following my recent breakup.

I take a moment to breathe in the fresh mountain air and allow the scent of hay and soil to fill my lungs. I'm an hour earlier than I thought I'd be: my Prius handled the winding mountain roads surprisingly well. I'm impressed.

Leaving my things in my car, I get out and decide to explore, walking around the side of the house, letting the tall grass caress my skin in the sunshine.

"Get ticks if y'all keep that up," a deep and raspy voice rumbles near me, making me jump.

That's when I see him.

He's on the back porch sitting in an old rocking chair, his bulky frame filling it to the point of overflowing. Even from this distance, I can see his strong jawline beneath handfuls of dark and graying scruff. He reminds me of a grizzly bear, especially with that scowl.

This *must* be Zeke, the grumpy gatekeeper himself, and thankfully not a grotesque soul-stealing demon after all... though I do understand now why his brother cautioned me about him.

"You lost?" he asks, and I swear his gravelly voice sounds as if he hasn't used it in days as it vibrates straight through my core.

Wait...what was that *about?*

"N-no, I'm... I mean... No, I'm not lost," I stammer, my confidence wavering under his intense gaze as I move away from the grass.

Blech! Ticks.

"Then why you roamin' around like you own the damn place?"

"I was just admiring your farm," I explain, lifting my chin, determined not to be intimidated. "Your brother Clay hired me."

"Hired you?"

"Yes, to help you while you recover," I say, eyeing the cast on his leg. Down by his feet a cute yellow lab reclines, pink tongue lolling out. A cane rests on the arm of the chair.

"Clay should mind his own business. I don't need no nurse," he mutters, shifting in his seat, his massive arms crossed over his broad chest.

"I'm *not* a nurse. I cook, clean, do laundry—but if you do need help with bathing, dressing, or using the restroom—"

"I can take care of myself," he says, cutting me off, his eyes narrowing.

I'm taken aback by his hostility. Then I remember what Clay said—Zeke needs help, whether he admits it or not.

"Well, I'm sorry, Mr. Radcliffe, but I'm here now, and I intend to do my job," I assert, my confidence growing.

His brow jumps briefly, then his scowl deepens. He rises from his chair with a noticeable wince, and I realize the man is not only broad, but tall. Well over six feet. He's rugged and imposing, and it sends a surprising flutter zinging through my belly. It's an odd, anxious tickle that rides the line between pleasant and uncomfortable. Like an itch I need to scratch.

Then he looks down at the dog and whistles loudly. "Get her, Peaches!"

The dog jumps up and barrels toward me. My heart stops.

But just as I turn to run, the dog skids to a halt, wagging its tail vigorously, and nuzzles my hand with a wet nose before flopping onto her back.

Yeah, real mean, this girl.

I laugh, bending down to give her belly a rub as she writhes happily on the ground.

"Your attack dog is called Peaches?" I call out with a smirk. "Seems pretty friendly to me."

Zeke grunts something unintelligible, his annoyance apparent as he hobbles over to lean on the porch railing. I stand, meeting his glare with what I hope is a winning smile.

There's a raw, unkempt allure to him, like an untamed wilderness. I can't help but be drawn to it. I study his face; the deep furrows of his scowl and the glint of determination in his blue eyes suggest a life of hard work and solitude.

He doesn't look at *all* like a cursed demon, actually. In fact, he reminds me of Hugh Jackman, at least when he's in Wolverine mode. A thicker, scruffier, angrier Wolverine. Yep. That's it.

His repeated refusals of help only fuel the spark of determination within me and make me all the more eager to take on a challenge.

"That wasn't very nice," I remark as I walk toward him. "Scare tactics are awfully juvenile."

He growls. "And your *attitude* is any better, nursey?"

Wow.

"Can we start over, then? Please? I'm Daisy Barnes. And I'll be staying here with you for a while, so I'd appreciate some respect."

"Respect?" He scoffs. "You'll get nothing but trouble around here, missy."

"Good thing I can handle trouble," I reply smoothly,

putting a hand on my hip. "And it's *Daisy*. Not missy. Not nursey."

He huffs. "I don't need no help. Especially from some young little...*thing* like you."

I shake my head. "Your brother thought it best for you to have some help to make sure you recover quickly."

He grumbles under his breath, his frustration evident. "I'm sick of all his fuss! Clay's worse than an old woman. I'm healing just fine on my own."

I raise an eyebrow, noticing the way he shifts his weight uncomfortably. "I guess we'll see, won't we? Whether you like it or not, I'm not going anywhere."

He stares me down, his piercing eyes burning with anger and...oh my, there's that tickle again. Then, without a word, he turns and hobbles slowly back into the house, the screen door slamming shut behind him. Peaches goes running after him, slipping in through the doggie door.

Well, Clay did mention Zeke was stubborn.

As I make my way to the front of the house, a truck pulls into the driveway. Another crazy tall man who looks like a slightly older and much less grumpy version of Zeke with a head of thick silver hair steps out, his expression growing concerned as he sees me. He marches toward the house, his pace quickening with each step.

"You must be Daisy! I'm Clay. You're a little early." He takes my hand in both of his warmly. "Thanks for coming."

"Very nice to meet you in person, Clay," I say with a smile. I gesture toward my car. "I was just about to—"

"Oh lord, you're not leaving, are you? Did Zeke give you that much of a hard time already?" Clay asks, dropping my hand hastily as worry creases his forehead.

"I'm not leaving." I smile and shake my head. "I just thought I'd get my bags from my car."

"Oh, thank heavens." He wipes his brow.

"But I *did* meet Zeke. And he's definitely...not happy."

He nods glumly. "I figured as much. Let me go talk to him. Then I'll come back and help you with your things."

"Thank you." I return to my car and grab two big duffle bags. When I reach the porch on the way back I can hear Zeke's protests through the farmhouse walls as he makes his feelings abundantly known to Clay. I sit on the bench out front to wait, and Peaches comes through the doggie door to keep me company. She sits by my side as my mind races with thoughts of my ex and the desperate situation that led me here. It's not like I could leave this place even if I wanted to. Where the hell would I go?

The slamming of a door inside the house signals the end of their discussion, and Clay emerges, wringing his large, calloused hands. "You're right, he's not happy. Just give him some time, Daisy. Please. He's... Well, he's got a lot to process. He's not used to needing help."

I nod, grateful not to be fired before I even start work. "Understood. I'll do my best."

Clay's expression softens, and he gives me a kind smile. "I'm sure you will. I'm glad you're here, Daisy."

As he heads to the car to grab a few more of my things, I enter the house and see Zeke making his way down a hallway, his movements slow and deliberate. I drop my duffle bags and walk closer to offer some assistance. "May I?"

"No need," he grunts, waving me off. "I can manage."

"Zeke. Let Daisy help," Clay interjects firmly as he maneuvers my stuff into the foyer. "She's here to make sure you don't further injure yourself. I need you back working in those fields as soon as possible."

Zeke glares at his brother defiantly but Clay remains steadfast, his gaze unwavering. I sense Zeke's reluctance to submit and can see that his pride is as substantial as his brawny physique. "Fine. But I won't be coddled. I'm just retirin' to my bedroom. Reckon I can manage *that* much on my own."

"Why don't you show Daisy to the guest room first, so she can settle in." Clay's voice is firm, leaving no room for argument.

Zeke's jaw clenches, his eyes darting between his brother and me. "This way," he finally grumbles, turning on his heel.

"I'll be back to check in on things tomorrow," Clay says with a smile before he leaves.

Zeke just grunts.

I wave goodbye to Clay before following Zeke, watching as he leans very heavily on the cane. Each step provides further evidence that his self-reliant bravado is just that—bravado.

I'm pressed close behind him in the tight space. Even hunched over to rely on the cane, he still fills the hallway. His broad, muscled back in its worn flannel shirt towers above me. He smells like laundry soap and a rich, clean, musk that has me drawing a deep breath. It's not at all what I imagined a laid-up farmer with a broken leg would smell like.

When he stops at an open doorway, I almost run into him.

"Your accommodations, m'lady," he declares with exaggerated flair. There's a hidden amusement in his tone. Had he been hoping to faze me with his sarcasm? Not happening, buddy.

I put a hand on his arm to squeeze past him into the room. Oh my...that arm is *solid*. The feel of it scrambles my brain for a moment, but I shake it off and take in the quaint, cozy room with its simple charm.

I let my gaze linger on the wrought-iron headboard, the flowery pattern on the quilt of the full-sized bed, and the gently distressed furniture around the room. The last light of the sun glows softly through the window. The room feels safe and calm. It's a pleasant contrast to my life lately.

I turn to Zeke and catch him openly assessing my figure, his eyes narrowed in unapologetic scrutiny. When he sees that he's busted he only grins wolfishly, suggesting he's trying anything he can to get me to quit.

Nice try.

He leans against the doorframe, filling the space with his overwhelming presence, his eyes never leaving mine. My pulse quickens, recognizing in our situation a second, unexpected challenge—one that affects my body as much as my mind.

"It's lovely," I say, chasing away those thoughts.

"It's the only guest room I got, so unless you'd like to bunk with me..." he offers, his face smug.

My cheeks burst into flame. *Damn it.* "N-no, thank you," I assure him. "This is perfectly fine."

He smirks. "Well, if you change your mind—"

"Mr. Radcliffe..." I warn.

He sighs. "You'll be dealing with things no self-respecting woman should have to with me. I think you can call me Zeke."

I chuckle. "Zeke, then."

"If you need...anything...just holler," he offers, his voice a low, rough whisper that sends a thrill down my spine in spite of myself. "I'm right across the hall."

I give him a curt but polite nod and shut the door, leaning against it. My heart is pounding, and I can't shake the feeling that this job—this *man*—is going to be a challenge unlike any other I've ever faced. But I'm ready to roll up my sleeves and prove to Zeke that sometimes even the strongest of men need a little saving.

CHAPTER 2
ZEKE

The invigorating aroma of fresh coffee invades my senses, nudging me awake.

It's an odd feeling, knowing that someone else is in *my* house, in *my* kitchen, making coffee like they own the place.

Daisy.

The ebony goddess hired to rob me of my pride.

For the record, I don't need takin' care of. Forget what Clay says. Sure, things aren't as easy as usual with this goddam cast on my leg, but I'm *not* an invalid. So what if I've been wallowing in self-pity since the day I broke the fool thing? The last thing I need is some young little beauty escorting me to the can. That'd just be another reminder of how old I'm gettin'.

I barely slept last night, my mind racing with thoughts of that gorgeous woman under my roof, and what I'd like to do to her sweet body. How did she manage to get under my skin so quickly, burrowing in like those ticks I warned her about? I don't know…maybe it's her determination, the way she looks at me with those big, warm eyes, it's…distracting.

I hobble into the kitchen after throwing on a pair of cargo shorts, T-shirt, and my favorite blue checkered flannel shirt.

My eyes land on Daisy immediately. She's washing dishes at the sink in leggings that make me want to take a big bite out of that juicy ass. She's found one of Ma's old aprons and has tied it around her waist. I didn't even realize I still had any of Ma's stuff kicking around, god rest her soul.

"Morning," she says, giving me a once over. Shoot, she's probably checking that I was able to dress myself properly. "Have a seat. Coffee?"

She pulls out a chair for me at the table and I sit down, even though I'm unwilling to do her bidding as easily as my dog…who's currently following her around like *she's* her mistress, I should add.

Peaches the traitor.

I nod and grunt a thanks as she sets a steaming mug in front of me, along with cream and sugar. I notice other delicious smells in the air besides the coffee—sweet and savory.

"Whatcha bakin'?" I ask.

She turns and throws a dish towel over her shoulder, a hand on her popped hip, and grins. "Banana nut muffins and some cheese and herb biscuits."

The oven timer dings and I instinctively start to get up to help her, but then remember I can't. Because I'm useless.

She goes over to take the food out of the oven and I have to admit, the muffins and biscuits look…delicious. Smell even better.

Fuck, even her coffee is better than mine.

I huff.

"I wanted to make eggs, too. But you're out. I'll have to run to the grocery store later today."

"We don't buy eggs, city girl," I scoff.

"Oh?" Her brow furrows uncertainly.

"Coop's right out back," I say brusquely. Maybe too brusquely. "Take that basket and collect some from the hens' nesting boxes. Just watch out for Harold." Harold is the meanest rooster you'll ever be unlucky enough to meet. I hope he'll teach this gal a lesson.

"Harold?" she asks, wiping her hands on the apron before removing it.

"My rooster. He's a menace on two spindly legs to anyone who dares venture into his territory."

She grabs the basket off the counter. "Is *he* the one that woke me up at 4:30 this morning?"

"Yup, that'd be him."

Her smile widens. "Then I've got a bone to pick with him anyway." If she wasn't so damn pretty, her gumption would be annoying.

She opens the screen door at the back. "How bad could it be? I'll be in and out before he even knows I'm there."

Famous last words, honey.

Daisy marches out purposefully, her chin high. As I observe her bold stride, I feel a twinge of guilt. Maybe sending her out to face Harold alone isn't the most honorable thing to do, but I'm curious to see how a city girl handles him. I lean on the counter as I peer through the kitchen window.

She enters the coop like a fearless lioness, but less than a minute later, there's a loud ruckus, and I'm tempted to hobble out there to run interference. But before I can do so, Daisy's sprinting out again in a zigzag pattern, her eyes wide with panic. Harold's hot on her heels, flapping his huge wings furiously.

"Stand your ground, girl!" I shout, not wanting her to get hurt. "Show him who's boss!" She stops and turns, planting her feet firmly, her chest rising and falling with each rapid breath. Harold, caught by surprise, slows his pursuit. "That's it. Keep starin' him down and then back away slowly," I instruct.

She does so, gradually retreating to the porch. Harold follows briefly, his bright red comb full, then with a final squawk of disgust he gives up and returns to his hens.

Daisy hustles into the kitchen, setting the egg basket on the counter before collapsing onto a chair, breathless and laughing.

"Now that's what I call a morning workout," she says, her voice filled with triumph and amusement.

I find myself laughing too. It's…been a while since I've done that.

She rolls up to her feet and stands close, playfully poking me in the chest. "You set me up, mister."

I hold my finger and thumb a quarter inch apart. "Maybe just a little."

"I figured." Her dark eyes flash as she studies me, her breath still labored.

It's hard to think with her in my space. She smells like coconut shampoo; a fresh, tropical scent that I hope still hangs in the air once she walks away.

"You did good," I mutter, sitting back down.

I catch her small smile as she turns her head briefly.

And my lonely heart swells.

Before suppertime, Daisy makes a trip to Nolan's General Store for some necessities, leaving me alone.

Frankly, not a moment too soon.

The woman follows me around like I'm a newborn calf on fresh legs. She even wanted to help me in the bathroom! I drew the line there, but I promised I'd text her if there was a problem.

I'll admit, it's nice having someone prepare my meals. But I hate everything else about this situation.

Well…mostly.

When she's gone, I settle into my rocking chair on the back porch, Peaches at my feet.

In the distance, I can see Clay coming in from the fields, his tall frame silhouetted by the golden wheat stalks like he's some damn superhero. He's been a know-it-all big brother since the day I was born, always one step ahead of me, or so he thinks.

"You didn't have to come, Clay," I grumble when he reaches the porch. "I don't need a babysitter."

"Easy there, Zeke. I'm just checking in, making sure you're not causing that poor girl too much trouble." He scratches his stubble, a smirk tugging at the corner of his mouth. "She seems nice. Pretty too, in a city kinda way. Just want to ensure you're being a gentleman."

I scoff, turning my head to hide the heat rising in my cheeks. "When have I *ever* been that?"

"True," he says, chuckling, then leaning on the railing.

"I don't need your advice on women. Besides, Daisy's our employee."

"But she won't be forever," he says. "If you don't make a move, maybe I will."

"You wouldn't dare," I growl, glaring at him. Peaches yips.

The thought of my brother and Daisy together makes me sick to my stomach.

He holds up his hands. "All right, all right. You know I'm just trying to get yer goat."

"Yeah, well, it worked," I huff. *Son of a bitch.*

He laughs. "Just looking out for you is all. For her, too. She's got fire in her eyes, but she still seems…vulnerable. Like life's knocked her down a peg, and you know the soft spot I have for the underdogs."

I relax, my anger deflating like a flat tire. Clay's always had a heart bigger than the Grand Canyon, and damn if it doesn't get to me sometimes. "Whaddya mean? What could possibly have happened to Daisy to have her feelin' like that?"

He shrugs. "I don't know the particulars. Just a feeling. But she seems like a good person, and maybe you owe it to her to be a little less...well...*you*."

I should fight him on this, but he's got a point. I'm not exactly easy to get along with.

Clay's voice breaks through my thoughts, and I realize he's *still* talking. "...And as far as the farm chores, Reece recommended a few guys from the ranch to help with the wheat harvest. And I already talked to Paige and a couple of her friends to lend a hand with the animals. So you can just focus on getting better...and giving Daisy less trouble."

I take a deep breath. "I'll try."

"That's all I'm asking." Clay slides off the railing and comes over to clap me on the shoulder, his tone softening. "Zeke... I know it's hard, but you'll be as good as new soon and back out there on the farm being your usual pain in the ass self."

I nod, unable to meet his gaze. Clay should understand better than anyone else how I feel, being three years older than me. As the years go by you start thinking about your mortality a lot more than when you're young. And with a hefty chunk of our youth spent taking care of our ailing parents rather than whooping it up out in the world, our lives have flown by.

If it means my brother will stop badgering me and start focusing on his own happiness, well, I reckon I can be a bit nicer to Daisy.

Just to get him off my back, of course.

CHAPTER 3
DAISY

The next few days on the farm aren't actually as difficult as I expected them to be. Zeke has become almost pleasant. He still grumbles at everything I ask of him, of course, trying to shoo me away or stare me down, much like Harold when I collect eggs from the coop.

But somehow it feels more like a game with Zeke than an actual standoff now. There's something *different* about how he looks at me.

Maybe I'm losing my mind, but I think I have a crush on the big bully.

Heaven help me.

Once I clean up after lunch, I sit down next to Zeke on the couch and eye him.

"That look is suspicious," he mutters.

"We need to work on the exercises the doctor gave you."

He closes his eyes and takes a breath. "Had a feelin' this was coming."

I arch a brow. "I saw you lifting those dumbbells in your bedroom. You're seriously strong up top. But you need to work your lower half, too. You don't want to end up like those meatheads that skip leg day."

He chews his lip. "Okay. Fine."

I unroll my yoga mat and ease him down onto it so he's lying flat on his back. I guide him through the prescribed stretches, sometimes touching him briefly to make sure he's maintaining proper form. His thick, bulging leg muscles flex and strain under the long basketball shorts as he tries to mask the pain with a stoic expression.

"You don't have to impress me, Zeke," I say. "If this hurts too much, tell me." My fingers brush against the bare skin of his thigh, sending a ripple of awareness through me.

"Don't flatter yourself," he grunts. "Not trying to impress nobody."

I chuckle. "Fine. Lift your leg higher, then," I instruct with a smirk. "And don't forget about your core." I put a hand on his belly, and he inhales quickly.

"This one always gets me," he grumbles, his leg muscles trembling. "Feelin' mighty pathetic, breaking a sweat just doing a few stretches."

"You have to work your way back to the *fine physique* you had before the accident," I say, smiling down at him. "And it's super important to maintain your flexibility, too." I shift further down his body. "Bend your knees and let's work on opening up those hips."

"Ain't nothin' wrong with those," he mutters.

"I didn't say there was, but I'm sure they're tight right now. Humor me?" I have him lift each leg one at a time and kick it to the side slowly. "Can you feel that?"

"Yep," he chokes, nodding quickly.

After a few reps, I tell him to curl his toes and then flex them, carefully, so as not to cause any cramping.

"Good. Now, lift this knee and let it fall over to the side, twisting your hips..." My fingertips glide over his knee. "Good job." I pat his flank, much too close to his rear end. *Oh god...*

I quickly pull away, my face flushing. "I didn't mean to—"

"Daisy darlin'," he says, stopping me in my tracks with that low, gravelly voice. His deep blue eyes meet mine, and he smirks. "If I'd known I'd get a pat on the rump doing these goddamn stretches, I woulda been doing them from day one."

I fight back a smile as I playfully smack his arm, then bury my head in my hands in embarrassment.

This man...

Then I feel his rough, calloused fingers on my wrist.

I jerk my head up.

"We gonna do the other side?" he says.

Oh. Yeah. Right.

"Of course." As I help him, my eyes glide over the bulge his shorts can't completely hide. I swallow, my throat suddenly dry, a shiver chasing down my spine.

It's difficult to conduct the remainder of the exercises completely professionally, knowing Zeke's aroused.

I take a steadying breath, reminding myself this is just another job. But Zeke Radcliffe is far from just another client. He's growing on me.

"That's enough for today," I announce, breaking the silence between us.

"I can keep goin'." His voice is rough.

"I'm sure you can, but you don't want to overdo it." I keep my tone light and clinical, even though I feel anything but.

He grunts in response, and I can't help but smile at his surly expression.

His thick brow arches. "Why are you here, Daisy?"

I sit up, folding my legs under me. "What do you mean? Your brother hired me."

He pushes up from the mat, propping himself up on his elbows, and I try not to notice the way his powerful chest rises and falls with each breath. "No, I mean where'd you work before here? And what had you comin' out to Deepwood Mountain at all? It ain't exactly the most happenin' place for a young lady." I can tell he's trying to keep his tone casual, but there's an edge to his voice. This isn't mere curiosity.

"I worked in Boise, for an HHA agency. But I had to leave the city for…personal reasons I'd rather not talk about."

His gaze intensifies, his blue eyes pinning me in place. "Tell ya what. You tell me what had you movin' to another state, and I'll tell you the embarrassin' story about breaking my leg."

My eyes widen. "Embarrassing? Clay told me you were fixing the farmhouse roof."

He averts his eyes momentarily. "Yeah, well, I had him swear on our parents' graves to keep quiet about it. Nobody else knows the actual story."

Wow. "Not even your doctor?"

"Nope."

I lick my lips. "You *are* upping the ante here. I mean, I'd have serious blackmail material."

He smirks. "Watch it, girl," he says with a smirk, and I love the way his mouth curves up. It's devilish and sexy and sends a jolt of electricity between my legs and—

Jeezus, Daisy.

"You have yourself a deal," I say, sitting up straighter.

"You gotta promise you'll keep it between yourself and the good lord above."

"Sure," I shrug.

"Naw, I need a spit shake on it."

"I'm sorry, a what-now?"

He looks incredulous. "You never heard of a spit shake?" He sits up, leaning toward me, and spits in his palm. Then he offers his hand. "Now you."

"You've got to be kidding me. That's..." I want to say disgusting, but I don't want to offend him. Is this something... *common* in these parts?

I spit—ugh—just barely, into my hand and take his. I'm *not* going to think about the warm glob of wetness between our palms.

Ewwww....

I hope my expression is neutral.

But it's obviously not. Zeke is laughing at me as he wipes his hand off on his shorts. "Wasn't *that* bad, was it?"

I wipe my own hand on my leggings. "N-not at all," I croak, then take a deep breath. "But this story better be worth it."

Zeke rolls onto his side on the mat. "I fell off the tractor."

I furrow my brow. "One of those huge ones that goes through the wheat fields? That's not embarrassing, that's horrifying!"

He shakes his head. "Naw. You can't fall off those unless you're an absolute moron and hanging off the outside. The operator's cab is enclosed."

"Then...?"

"I was on one of the smaller ones we use for haulin' hay and pullin' shit around the farm."

"What happened?"

"I turned to yell at a damn goat that'd gotten into the feed room and ran into a tree. Tumbled right off and onto my leg."

I can't help but grin, imagining Zeke telling off a goat one second and hitting the ground the next.

"There's more..." He squints, looking away from me. "I landed in a *steaming* cow pie."

"Oh my god." I start giggling.

"And I had to lie there waiting for Clay while that fucking goat licked my face."

I cover my mouth and laugh, picturing Zeke on the ground, raging *and* stinking to high heaven, even as a goat tortured him with licks.

"If this gets out, I'll never hear the end of it." A slight blush creeps up his neck. "It'll ruin my reputation and all."

"As what? The grumpiest farmer in town?" I tease.

His eyes narrow playfully. "Careful, city girl. You can only poke the bear so many times before he attacks."

"I'm confident I can outrun this bear."

He rolls his eyes. "Yeah, for now," he says, and my cheeks heat. Maybe that was a little too on the nose. "Okay, your turn. I want to know how a pretty young home health aide came to wander into my yard."

The compliment catches me off guard. "You don't have to flirt to get me to keep your secrets, Zeke. I already agreed to that. With spit, even."

I eye my hand dubiously, and he grins.

"Ain't flirtin', silly girl. But you better get talkin', or else."

"Or else what?"

Zeke's eyes sparkle as his eyes roam over me, slowly.

My mind whirls and I hurry to move on to fill the awkward silence. "My ex-boyfriend kicked me out of the house."

Immediately, Zeke's demeanor changes.

"He *what*?!" he booms, and Peaches races in from the porch with a whine and lies down near us.

"He..." I pull my knees up to hug them. "He met someone else and told me to leave. Said he wasn't in love with me anymore."

He sits up, nostrils flaring, chest heaving. "Did you know he was cheatin'?"

"Deep down...maybe. There were signs." I shrug. "Turns out it was another home health aide I worked with at the agency."

Kelly. And I thought she was my friend.

"Well, fuck me."

"Yeah... It was a shock."

"But why'd you leave the agency?"

I huff. "He's the owner."

He growls. "That piece of *shit*."

I reach out and touch Zeke's knee, my touch reassuring. "It's been over a month. I'm over it. No use wasting time thinking about douchebags. That's why I don't like to talk about it. I don't want him taking up space in my brain anymore, you know?"

"Good riddance." He looks at my hand. "It's just...a dick move. He deserves to be held accountable for treatin' you that way."

I smile. "I'm counting on karma to do that for me."

"I was thinking more like tossin' him in the hay baler..."

"*Zeke!*"

"I'm jokin', I'm jokin'," he grumbles. He squints at me. "Sorta."

I laugh and squeeze his knee. "Thank you."

His blue eyes soften, and I melt.

I have to admit, it feels kind of nice to have the gruff farmer so clearly in my corner. My ex never showed any inkling of protectiveness toward me. I guess he would have had to love me enough to care like that. I don't think that was ever the case.

When I go to bed that night, Zeke is right there in my dreams, growling at my ex, guarding me with his thick body, protecting me like a big, angry dragon would his precious hoard. And when my hand slips into my panties, I picture Zeke whispering sweet words in that deep, raspy voice against my ear, taking me higher and higher, until I'm a shaking, breathless mess in the sheets, moaning his name as I come.

What am I going to do?

CHAPTER 4
ZEKE

Daisy's been strangely quiet all day. Barely looked me in the eye.

I don't like it. I've gotten used to her sharp tongue, not to mention her smiles.

I'm still madder than a hornet in a soda can hearing what that lowlife ex of hers did. How could anyone treat Daisy like that? She's the sweetest woman I've ever met, even if she can be a right nag when it comes to my exercises. She deserves so much better.

Just as I'm heading out to the porch to enjoy the sunset, Daisy walks in from the bathroom.

"It's bath day, Zeke."

Is she serious? "I don't recall discussin' this."

"There's nothing to discuss. You need one. Let's go." She crosses her arms over her chest. I can't help eying her cleavage in her halter top.

"You gonna take one with me?" I ask, before I can stop myself. Too late. It's out there.

She closes her eyes and shakes her head. "No," she says firmly, but there's a rosiness in her cheeks that wasn't there before. Is she embarrassed that I'm asking? Or is there a part of her that likes the idea? "Go take off your clothes and put this towel around your waist, please."

If those words came out of her mouth under any other circumstances, I'd be on board. But a bath? "I wash all the important parts every day. Don't need a whole bath to get clean."

"It's not just to get clean. Baths relax tense muscles, stimulate the nervous system, and exfoliate your skin. Come on, you'll enjoy it. I can scrub your back?"

Yeah, that's what I'm afraid of. She's gonna touch me and I'm gonna grow some major wood with nowhere to hide it.

"Fine, my back. But I don't need you to bathe the rest of me," I mutter, putting on my best scowl.

"If you say so," she says, with a smirk.

After I change, with only a flimsy towel around my waist and murmuring a prayer that it doesn't fall off as I limp along, I enter the bathroom. My ancient but sturdy clawfoot tub is filled with mountains of bubbles. Steam from the water, scented with lavender, hangs about the room.

"I'm gonna smell like dear old Ma, god rest her soul," I say, hobbling over.

Daisy turns and I swear her rich, dark eyes rove over my bare body longer than necessary. Does she like what she sees? I'm big, heftier than some of the other guys in Deepwood. Barrel-chested, not lean.

"Oh...um... Sorry, that's all I could find," she says, her cheeks a little flushed. "Next time I'm at Nolan's I'll see if Griff has something more masculine smelling."

She guides me to a chair set up near the tub and kneels to put on the cast cover. As she secures it near my knee, I'm painfully aware how close she is to my bare thighs and my cock—which has got a jump on me. I will away my growing erection as best I can. *It's just a bath. Like you used to give Ma when she got sick.*

There we go. Nothing like thinking about your ma to make your dick go limp.

"Sit on the edge of the tub and put your good leg in. Then use me to lower yourself. I'll turn my head so you can remove your towel. Just let me know when you're in the water."

"You sure you don't want to take a peek?" I say. God help me, I wouldn't know what to do if she said yes.

"Zeke..." she warns.

"Yeah, yeah..." I reply, flinging the towel to the side, then lowering myself into the water.

She's added a ledge to the tub on the cast side, and I prop my leg up on it. When the rest of me is submerged, the bubbles covering my crotch, I tell her.

"It's safe to look now."

She chuckles. "How's the water?"

"Nice," I say, the hot water soothing my muscles. Dammit, why does she have to be right all the time?

"Good," she smiles, handing me a washcloth and soap.

I get to work scrubbing my face, my arms, my underarms and chest.

"Okay, this feels...not terrible," I grudgingly admit.

"I thought you'd enjoy it. How long has it been since you've had a proper shower or bath?"

I purse my lips and look up to the ceiling, thinking. Was it three weeks? Four?

"Yeah, if you can't remember, it's been too long." I roll my eyes.

She angles the chair behind me and works some soap into a sponge. The moment she drags it along my back and shoulders, I'm a goner.

I let out a deep groan, the steam rising up to envelop my

face. It feels much too good to have her hands on me, scrubbing my back and sending tingles to every nerve ending.

"You're really good at this, Daisy," I murmur, my voice rumbling in my chest.

Our eyes meet in the mirror on the wall, the steam swirling around us. She smiles. "Thank you," she says softly. "I'm just doing my job."

But it's got to be more than that, I can feel it in her touch.

"Is it—is it difficult?" I ask, as she squeezes some shampoo into her hand. "Being a long-term caregiver, I mean. It must take the patience of a saint. Especially when you have pain-in-the-ass clients like me."

She chuckles. "It can be tough, but it's rewarding, too. I like helping people. My mom was the same. She always had a way with people."

I nod, my eyes fixed on the floor. "I know I give Clay a hard time, but it's family that sticks by you through thick and thin. I shouldn't take him for granted, but I think I do."

She begins washing my hair, sending a whole new set of tingles over my scalp and down my neck.

"How so?" she asks.

I shift, the water lapping at my chest. "When I was younger, my folks got sick. Like, real sick. Clay had just joined the Marines, so I had to take care of 'em all on my own. Look after the farm, too."

She pauses and drops a hand to my shoulder.

"I was just a kid, ya know? But I managed. That's where I learned the value of hard work and independence. Didn't want nobody's help 'cause I thought I could do it all. Still can, most days. When I'm not laid up with my leg in a damn cast, that is."

She rubs my shoulder. "That's a lot for a teenager to

handle. I can see why you're so self-reliant. But you know, sometimes it's okay to let people in, to let them help you."

I shrug. "I don't want to burden Clay. That's why I don't like him comin' around. I want him outta my business so he can tend to his own."

"But he's family, Zeke. And you said it yourself: family's important."

"Why you gotta be so damn smart all the time?" I ask as she starts rinsing my hair. "You ain't like any of the other women I've ever met. You don't take no crap. Especially mine."

She laughs. "Your crap isn't so bad."

I reach up and put my hand over hers on my shoulder. "Good, because as much as I bitch and complain, I kinda like having you here."

Her voice is barely a whisper when she replies. "I kinda like being here with you, too."

I smile, and there's a flutter in my belly to think she doesn't hate me.

After a few moments, she helps me up and gives me a fresh towel to dry myself. She removes the cast cover and guides me to my bedroom, where she turns her head while I put on clean shorts.

"Have a seat—I want to put some lotion on you to help with that dry skin," she says, grabbing a pump bottle.

My stomach clenches at the idea of her rubbing lotion into my body. No big deal. Just relax and—

Holy mother of god…

And I thought the sponge was nice!

This… This is heaven. Her hands slide over my neck and shoulders first, and I'm having the hardest time not melting into a puddle right there on the bed.

"You can get down on your stomach for now. I'll flip you over when it's time to do the front."

Front?

Oh, hell.

She makes her way down my back, finding sore muscles that ache for her touch. Those groans must be coming from me, but honestly, I feel like I'm in another world.

As she works on my hamstrings, I have to stuff the pillow in my mouth to stop sounding like a porn star. And when her fingers touch my feet, sliding in between my toes and tracing the lines of my arches, I realize how much of an erogenous zone they really are for me. I don't want her ever to stop as she rubs each toe on my foot peeking out of the cast. It's like a month-long itch that needs to be scratched.

She turns me over, and I'm sure she'll notice my raging hard-on.

How can she not?

But she doesn't say a word, just takes her time, slowly driving me insane as she applies lotion to my arms and chest. She's careful to avoid my nipples, which only makes me want her to touch them more. And I know she can feel my stomach muscles contract with every swipe of her hands over my belly.

By the time she finishes, my heart is pounding, and I'm hyper aware of the elephant—or is that elephant *trunk*—in the room. I can hear her ragged breathing, and I wonder if she's turned on, too.

"There…um…all set. I'll leave you to rest."

I grab her wrist. "Daisy, wait…"

Her fingers freeze on the comforter. She wets her lips, making me want to groan all over again. Her gaze holds mine, and I see the unspoken question hanging there. But before I can say or do anything, we're interrupted by the bellowing sound of Clay's voice. "Zeke! Daisy!"

"In my bedroom!" I holler back, throwing the edge of the comforter over my bulge.

Clay tears into the room. He looks frantic.

"The east field's burning. The fire department's heading here now. When I know more I'll call you."

I go to slide off the bed. "The hell with that. I'm coming with you."

"No you're not. You're stayin' put." Clay looks at Daisy. "Don't let him go anywhere."

"Clay!" I yell as he runs out the door.

I stand, looking around for my cane.

"Bring me my cane, Daisy. We're going."

She shakes her head. "Sorry, no. You're not going anywhere."

I throw the bottle of lotion at the wall. "Take me. Now!"

Her eyes flash. "You're going to throw a tantrum like a child? Really?"

I glare at her. Why does her fiery determination ignite such a flame within me? She stands her ground, those deep brown eyes unwavering, daring me to defy her.

"You're still healing, Zeke. Running around on that leg could re-injure it, setting you back weeks. Do you really want to risk more time away from your work?" Daisy's voice is firm but laced with that goddamn sweet concern I've come to crave. "Let the firefighters and Clay handle this. You've just gotta be patient."

Patient? Me? I've never been good at waiting, especially when the farm is concerned. I grit my teeth, feeling the all-too-familiar frustration at my helplessness wash over me. "Dammit, Daisy, I can't just sit here while my land burns." I try to keep my voice even, but it comes out as a raw, low growl.

She takes a step closer, confronting my anger unflinchingly.

I both hate and love that about her. "Well, you can't do much on a broken leg, can you? You'd only get in the way."

Her words cut deep, wounding my primitive male pride. "I'm still a man, Daisy," I snarl. "Just 'cause I'm laid up—"

"If you can't fight a fire, what *else* could you do to make you feel like more of a man?" She takes another step, so close now that I can feel the heat of her breath on my face. There's a glint in her eye that tells me she understands my struggle, even as she challenges it.

Before I can respond, she continues, her voice husky. "Show me, Zeke. Show me how much of a man you are."

Her whispered invitation is my undoing. I reach out, my big hand curling around the back of her slender neck. I force her back against the wall, pressing my bulky body against hers. She doesn't resist; instead, she rises onto her toes, meeting my lips with her own.

The kiss is immediate and explosive, a collision of our passions. I taste her heat as she responds with an eagerness that matches my own. She moans into my mouth, her hands clawing at my chest, her searing, demanding touch igniting a blaze in my body that rivals the fire outside.

I deepen the kiss, my tongue sweeping into her mouth, claiming her with a possessiveness that shocks me. But she doesn't pull away: she meets my fervor with an equal measure of hunger. Our tongues explore together as I let out a moan that comes from the depths of my soul.

My heart pounds, the rhythm matching the heavy throb between my thighs. I want her—need her to ease this ache. Her body fits with mine like a missing puzzle piece, soft curves against hard muscle, and I feel every inch of her, a tantalizing tease for my desperate cock.

We break apart, both gasping for air. I lift her chin up with my fingertip, staring down into her dark eyes.

"Damn, woman, you are a firecracker," I mutter, voice hoarse.

Daisy smiles seductively, curving her full lips, and my resolve shatters further. "Maybe I should just stay right here. Let the fire outside burn itself out," I joke.

She chuckles. "I know you don't really mean that. But it's quite the compliment, thank you."

Her hands slide up my chest, and I seek out her mouth again. I nip at her lips, then slide my tongue against hers, pouring every ounce of my pent-up desire into her. She grinds against me, driving me insane. I growl, my cock on the edge of exploding in my shorts.

And then my phone rings.

I let out a frustrated groan.

Daisy sinks back against the wall. "That's probably Clay."

"Damn bastard's always interruptin'," I huff, and give her a kiss on the forehead before hobbling over to pick up the phone. "What is it?" I answer.

"Firefighters almost got it completely contained. It's about a quarter of the east field." Clay pauses. "Not great, Zeke. But not terrible, either."

Thank god. "That's...good news. Thanks, Clay."

"*Thanks*? What's gotten into you? Daisy give you some kind of sedative or somethin'?"

I chuckle and look over at Daisy. "Somethin' like that, yeah."

"Well, keep your phone close and I'll give you more updates as they happen."

"Will do."

I hang up and take a seat on the bed. "Fire's pretty much contained. Damage isn't horrible."

"Oh, that's good news."

I nod. "He'll be callin' me with updates."

She smiles and bites her lush bottom lip that I was tasting just moments ago. "I should probably go to bed, Zeke. You have a lot to deal with tonight."

I guess she's right. Always the practical one. "Well, if you're sure. Night, Daisy."

And I watch her leave my bedroom, my body aching for her.

CHAPTER 5
DAISY

The sun seems to have forgotten that fall is upon us, and heat beats down on my back as I pluck weeds from the small vegetable garden. Who knew this city girl's favorite spot on the farm would be crawling around in the dirt with the plants? But it's a place of peace and quiet for me, somewhere I can escape for a little while to be alone with my thoughts.

Thoughts of Zeke...and how his hands and mouth and body felt on mine when he kissed me last night.

I've never felt that kind of raw, wild sexuality.

I know I encouraged him. How could I not? The ache inside me had grown to the point that I had no choice but to distract him from his frustration at being unable to go with Clay. And what a distraction it was...

I squeeze my thighs together just thinking about it. I swear, I've been wet ever since. So when Zeke left early with Clay to survey the fire damage in the daylight, I decided to come out here to think about why I didn't stay with him last night.

"Daisy?" a voice calls, snatching me from my thoughts.

Peaches barks from beside me, instantly on high alert.

Standing up, brushing dirt from my palms, I spot my ex,

Theo, striding toward me with his all-too-familiar arrogance I'd thought I'd said goodbye to. I realize it's the first time I've laid eyes on him since he threw all my belongings out on the street. How the hell did he find me here, anyway?

"What are you doing here, Theo?" I ask, my tone cold.

He has the audacity to smile, a smile I once thought charming but now appears more like a smug grin. "I'll cut to the chase, so we can get out of this... place." His eyes scan the farm with obvious condescension. "I made a mistake letting you go, sweetheart. I want you back."

Sweetheart? The word sounds foreign in my ear, like a favorite dish that now tastes bitter.

I huff. "I don't understand. A few weeks ago, I was an inconvenience in your life. Now suddenly you want me back?"

Theo's eyes dart away, and in that moment I realize that Kelly must have kicked him to the curb.

"Things change. I realize now the treasure I had in you. Come back home with me, Daisy. You can have your old job back, maybe even more. We can start a new chapter together... talk about marriage...maybe a family."

Laughter bubbles up from my throat, a mixture of disbelief and genuine amusement. "What happened to Kelly?"

His smile falters. "She just wasn't the one for me, babe."

"Wow. I see. When it doesn't work out with your flavor of the month, you come crawling back. Sorry, Theo, you only get one chance to go on this ride and you blew it."

He pauses, but then alters his expression. "I'm serious, Daisy. You know I can give you a more comfortable life than *this*." He gestures around at the farm, his nose wrinkling slightly.

"I don't want your life anymore, Theo. I want this." My hand sweeps across the land, the fields, the barn, and the farmhouse that already feel like home. "I've learned to appreciate what's real and genuine, not the flashy, superficial existence I had with you."

The lines of his face harden, his eyes narrowed into angry slits. "Is this about that crippled farmer?"

Disgusting. Imagine if his staff and clients heard him calling the very people they help such names! "Zeke's more of a man than you'll ever be, Theo. He'd never treat someone the way you treated me."

Theo's face turns as red as the tomatoes ripening in the garden. "Wow, you've got it bad. I can see it in your eyes. Well, enjoy your little fling while it lasts. Once his leg heals, he'll be off to the next farmgirl."

"Get out, Theo! You have no right to be here, and you have less than zero idea what you're talking about."

Before Theo can say another word, the screen door on the back porch bangs open and then slams shut again.

"Who the hell are you?" Zeke's deep voice rumbles.

I smile at the sight of him hobbling down the porch steps, making his way over to us, and the way the sun behind him outlines his broad frame makes my chest tighten.

"It's just my ex," I answer, watching as recognition dawns on Zeke's face, an angry glint entering his eye.

"What are you doing on my property?" Zeke's voice, already gravelly, takes on an even darker edge, each word laced with threat.

Theo stands taller, his teeth flashing. "I came to get Daisy, of course. I'm here to take her back where she belongs."

Zeke's face twists into a dangerous scowl. "No. She'll be stayin' here with me from here on out, understand? Go on—git —and don't ever come back." Zeke reaches into his pocket, and for a heart-stopping moment I think he might have a weapon. Theo must think the same thing because he takes a hasty step back, hands held up in surrender.

But it's just Zeke's phone. He taps something on it and then slides it back into his shorts pocket. He smirks, thumping his cane hard against the ground, eyes locked on Theo. Nice bluff.

"You don't scare me, you big redneck," Theo spits, his false bravado returning. "Daisy, tell this fucking hillbilly to back off!"

"I'm not telling him anything, Theo," I say coolly.

Theo marches right up to Zeke, desperately trying to get his eyes level with Zeke's. But with their height difference... well, it's comical, really.

Zeke shakes his head, almost laughing in Theo's face. "She's with me now, so why don't you just run along back to your pathetic excuse for a life?"

Theo's eyes flash to mine, then he spits on the ground. "Stupid whore," he says, his voice low. His gaze flicks back to Zeke. "She doesn't know what she's missing, sticking around here with a broken-down old—"

Zeke doesn't let him finish. He swings his cane, clipping Theo hard on the side of the knee, sending him howling to the ground.

"I think I made myself clear, you piece of shit. Now get off my property before I go and get my gun."

Theo scrambles to his feet, massaging his throbbing knee. "You're fucking crazy, asshole," he yells at Zeke. "You know what? You can have her." Then he turns to me, eyes filled with hatred. "You'll be crawling back in less than a month, bitch."

Zeke steps forward at that, and Theo jumps before storming off. I feel a rush of emotions—anger, relief, pride. Zeke wants me to stay. And he's willing to fight for me.

I run up to him and wrap my arms around him tight. His body is still shaking, breath labored from the exertion, fists clenching and unclenching at his sides.

"I won't ever let that bastard hurt you, Daisy," he says, his arms coming around to hold me in a protective embrace. I tilt my head up and see a storm raging in his eyes, mirroring the turbulent feelings inside me. "He doesn't deserve you."

"Thank you. For standing up for me."

A sizzle of electricity runs between us. "I wasn't going to let him walk all over you like that."

Our eyes lock, and I'm lost in their blue pools. This mean ole brute of a farmer has shown me more respect and consideration than Theo ever did.

"I want to be yours, Zeke," I blurt out, surprised at the words tumbling from my lips. His eyes widen, mirroring my shock. "I mean...I...uh..." I sputter, suddenly feeling heat spreading over my cheeks.

Instead of laughing or brushing off my confession, Zeke tightens his grip on me. He cups the back of my neck and leans down to press his lips against mine, warm and firm, but gentle. I melt into him, savoring the passion and the tenderness.

"And I want to be yours," he says, momentarily breaking the kiss, then diving back in with more ferocity. This kiss is a possessive promise of what he wants to give me, and it fills me with sweet longing.

As our lips part, Zeke's thumb sweeps across my bottom lip. "I need you, Daisy. Now."

I swallow at the desperation in his voice and pull him toward the porch.

It takes us *much* too long to get to the kitchen, where Zeke pulls me against him and kisses me deeply, his big hands kneading my behind. "God, this ass is fine."

I whimper as his cock prods at my hip, hard and heavy.

By the time we finally make it to the bedroom I'm trembling with anticipation, my fingers tugging at the buttons on his shirt, desperate to feel his skin against mine. I can see the desire blazing in his eyes too, his gruffness now directed at our clothes and how annoyingly in the way they are.

"I don't want to waste a second more," I whisper, pushing his shirt off his broad shoulders. I push up his T-shirt, pressing urgent kisses to his barreled chest. I can feel his heartbeat under my lips, erratic and fast.

He groans and pulls his T-shirt up and over his head, tossing it aside. His hands slide down my back, pressing me against the massive length in his cargo shorts. I let my head tip back, gasping at the sheer size of him, and Zeke takes that opportunity to trail his lips along my jaw and down my neck, his hot breath sending shudders through me. "You're so beautiful," he breathes, his voice hoarse with want. "I've dreamed of this."

"Of us?" I ask, my body writhing against his.

"Yes. And of tasting every inch of you," he murmurs, his lips curving against my collarbone.

I chuckle. "Who knew the grumpy farmer would be such a charmer?"

"There's a lot you don't know about me, Daisy Barnes." His blue eyes flash before he pushes me back onto the bed and climbs over me, being careful of his cast. His body is a delicious cage as he looms over me. "Why don't you let me show you."

With swift, practiced movements, he unbuttons my top and reveals my bra. He trails his rough fingers over the edges of the lace, teasing my skin. My breath comes faster as he undoes the front clasp and pushes the fabric aside. "These breasts..." He brushes his fingers over my pebbled nipples, circling them with a soft, tantalizing touch. Then he lowers his head and worships my body with his mouth, tongue, and teeth. I arch into him, and gasp.

"Mmmm… they're like two delicious ice cream sundaes with tart little cherries on top. My *favorite* dessert."

I moan, threading my fingers through his hair. "Zeke," I whisper, as he moves down, planting a line of kisses along my belly, making me squirm. The sensation of his scruffy chin on my skin is only turning me on more. When he reaches the waist of my jeans, he pops the button and unzips them slowly. Then he leans back and slides them down and off my legs with deliberate care.

I'm left in only my panties.

He slides his fingers over the fabric. "Damn, Daisy, you're so wet."

"I've been wet nonstop, thinking about you."

He groans. "Oh, hon, then why didn't you stay with me last night?"

I run my fingers over his stubbled cheek. "You had other things to worry about. I didn't want to get in the way of that."

"You're never in the way. You're the only thing that really matters. The farm, my property…in the end, it's all pointless without you. Everything else can go to hell."

I smile as he takes my fingers and kisses them one by one. This man is amazing. "Help me get these panties off, will you?"

"Yes, Ma'am."

I lift my hips and he slides my underwear down my legs until I can kick them away.

Once I'm bare before him, he leans back, drinking me in. "Daisy, you're the sexiest thing I've ever seen."

I love how beautiful and desired his words make me feel. I reach out and move his hands to my pussy. "Touch me…"

He bites his lip and strokes over my slick folds. "*Fuck*…I… I need to taste you, honey." He drops to his side and rolls onto his back. "Straddle my face."

My eyes go wide. "Uh… Okay. If you're sure."

"I've never been more sure of anythin'," he says with a wolfish grin.

I sit up and remove my top and bra completely, then begin to position myself over his head.

"Other way, darlin'. I want you facin' my feet."

I blink. I've never done anything like this, but I'm not averse to the idea. In fact, my stomach clenches in anticipation just thinking about it.

I turn and place a palm on either side of Zeke's belly, lowering my hips.

His hot breath hits my pussy, and I gasp. "Zeke, yes," I moan, already lost in the pleasure he's about to give me. When his mouth touches me, I cry out loud enough for the goats in the barn to hear.

In an instant, he's stroking, licking, and sucking in all the right places. I clutch at the comforter, my hips naturally moving in time with his rhythm. Each flick of his tongue sends sparks of pleasure through my core, building an exquisite tension. I moan, and gasp, and cry out his name, my voice breathy and desperate.

"Don't stop," I beg, bucking my hips slightly. "Don't ever stop."

Zeke groans. "Not in a million years," he says, his words vibrating through me. His hands grip my thighs, holding me in place as his skilled tongue works its magic, stripping me bare in every way.

My body begins to shake and in seconds, his expert tongue has me sailing over the edge. I cry out, my body trembling as my orgasm rips through me.

I'm utterly at his mercy as he holds my thighs apart, continuing to work my pussy as the waves of pleasure subside.

I crawl forward, unbuttoning his shorts, desperate to release the monstrous cock still trapped beneath *far* too much material.

He lifts his hips and I push his clothes down but not off. His erection juts right into my face. "I think this big monster needs some love," I say, grasping it in my hand.

"God yes..." Zeke moans. "Go ahead. I'm enjoyin' the view."

I chuckle, knowing my ass is directly in front of him.

I lean forward. "You are so hard," I say, placing a kiss on his tip, then running my fingertip over it, massaging in the slick pre-cum.

His breath catches and his body arches up into me.

"Easy there, sexy," I tease, my breath hot on his skin. I take him into my mouth slowly, savoring his taste, feeling him throb.

Zeke lets out a ragged groan and his hands grasp my hips, his body taut with restraint. "Damn, woman... That feels like heaven."

I hum around his cock, the vibrations making his hips twitch and buck slightly. Then I pull back, dragging my tongue along his shaft. "Yeah? You like that?" I murmur as he squeezes my ass cheeks.

He gasps frantically. "Yeah...yeah, I do." He's panting now, his chest heaving with the effort to stay still.

I take him deep once more, using my hand to stroke the part of his cock I can't reach with my mouth, which is a lot. The man is huge. I set a steady, rhythmic pace, my tongue swirling, his salty pre-cum an addictive treat. I love the way he tastes, the way he responds to my every touch.

"*Oh...oh god, Daisy,*" he gasps, his hips thrusting upward, seeking more friction. I can feel his control slipping.

"No, Daisy…please. Stop. I want to come inside your pussy," he pants, and I reluctantly slide off his cock.

"I didn't want to stop…" I say, turning around to face him.

He smiles. "Hell, that was the hardest thing I've had to say in a long time."

I laugh, running my hands over his broad chest, my nails dragging over his skin.

"Ahh…yes…" he groans.

I take my time exploring his body, kissing and nipping at his torso, reveling in the feel of his heated flesh under my fingers and lips. I suck his nipples into my mouth, enjoying the way he squirms underneath me.

"You're a little devil," he growls playfully.

I chuckle again, sitting up to straddle him, my center hovering above his thick shaft. "You ready to fuck me, Zeke?"

His brow furrows. "I don't have any condoms, but it's been a while since I've seen any action."

"I was tested after Theo to make sure he didn't give me anything, and I'm on the pill."

"If you're happy with that, then saddle up," he says, swatting my ass.

I waggle my eyebrows. "It's a mighty big saddle," I say, guiding him to my entrance. "But I'm game to ride it." I tease us for a moment, rubbing his tip along my slick folds. Zeke groans, his hands grasping my hips as I lower myself onto him inch by delicious inch.

When he's fully seated in me I remain still, adjusting to his impressive size, relishing the way he fills me.

"Baby, you fit me like a glove," Zeke says, his head falling back on the bed.

I begin to move, setting a pace that has him gritting his teeth with pleasure. His hands roam all over my body, cupping and squeezing my breasts and pinching my nipples before sliding down to grip my ass, urging me on.

"That's it, Daisy. Ride me. Just like that. Fuck, just like that…" His voice is hoarse, his blue eyes intense as they watch me.

I lean forward, my breasts brushing his chest as I quicken my pace, the bed creaking beneath us. I'm so close. My muscles begin to quiver.

"Zeke," I breathe, nails digging into his chest. "I'm—"

"Me too," he grunts, his jaw clenched.

I pour every ounce of my soul into my movements, and he rises to meet me, his hips thrusting up as I descend, our bodies slamming together. I shout, my release exploding through me, and when Zeke joins me, a booming roar rumbles from deep within his chest.

We shake, our bodies jerking and convulsing together, and I collapse onto his sweat-slicked chest. He wraps his arms around me, holding me tight as our hearts pound in a synchronized rhythm.

"If it's this incredible with a cast on my leg," he laughs, "I can't *wait* until I'm fully healed."

I laugh back, happy and carefree. I haven't felt this way in a long, long time.

Who knew I'd find it again all the way out here on a farm run by a grumpy, sexy-as-hell farmer on the outskirts of Deepwood Mountain?

CHAPTER 6
ZEKE

With one last fond look at Daisy sleeping like the dead in my bed, I creep through the bedroom to the kitchen.

As well I can creep with a cane and a cast, that is.

Last night was…incredible, losing myself in that bonfire of a woman, discovering passion I never knew could exist.

And now I'm totally ravenous.

I figure cooking a hearty breakfast for us is the right thing to do. I want to take care of her, show her that I can still be useful, even with this damn leg.

I hobble toward the back door, wincing at the stiffness in my muscles after our night of…let's just say, *exertion*. The chickens are already awake, their soft clucks and chirps filling the cool morning air. As I enter the coop Harold eyes me. He knows I don't take shit from him. He just struts on by as I collect the eggs in the basket.

I'm already picturing the look on Daisy's sweet face when she sees the feast I'm gonna prepare for her.

And that's when my foot catches on the uneven ground, and I stumble.

"Damn it!" I roar as I tumble to the ground. The eggs fly out of the basket and crack, their yolks staining the dirt, and I land with a heavy thud on my ass, my injured leg throbbing from the impact.

"*Son of a...*" I grunt, my frustration turning to anger.

I sit there simmering as Peaches comes running over, her tail wagging eagerly. It's like she's excited by my misfortune, the little weirdo.

"Go away, girl," I mutter, shoving her away. I don't want anyone seeing me like this, not even the damn dog.

Just as I begin to push myself up, I hear Daisy's voice calling from the house. "Zeke? Are you all right?"

I freeze. I don't want her seeing me weak and helpless like this, especially after last night. But before I can say a word, Peaches goes barreling back toward the house, her nails clicking on the wooden porch. I curse, knowing Daisy will be on her way.

Sure enough, she appears in the doorway of the coop, her eyes wide. "Zeke! What happened? Are you hurt?" She rushes to my side, her hands hesitant, as if she's unsure whether to touch me or not.

I wave her off, my pride still stinging from the fall. "I'm fine, just fine." I struggle to stand, gritting my teeth against the pain. "It's nothin'. Just a little stumble. I'll be inside in a minute."

Daisy is insistent. "Let me help you," she says, her voice soft yet firm. I can see the worry in her eyes, and it only makes me angrier.

"I don't need any help, woman," I snap, my frustration getting the better of me. "I'm burden enough already. Can't even make a simple breakfast without breakin' another fucking leg!" My voice grows louder with each word, the anger bubbling in my chest.

Daisy doesn't flinch; instead, she kneels in front of me and sits back on her heels. "You're *not* a burden, Zeke. And I don't want you thinking that way. I'm not going anywhere, you hear?" There's steel in her voice, and dammit, if it doesn't turn me on.

I huff. "I'm just... worried. Even after I heal up, I'll still be an old man. More useless with every day that passes. You need someone younger, stronger. Someone who can take care of you." The words taste like bile in my mouth as I say them.

"Enough." She pulls away, her eyes narrowing on me. "You listen here, Zeke," she says, her voice low and measured. "I'm not going anywhere. I don't want some immature kid; I want *you*. I can handle myself, and I can handle *you*, broken leg and all. So stop pushing me away. I'm here to stay."

Her words strike a chord deep within me, warming my cold, gruff heart. I reach out and take her hand, pulling her close despite the pain in my leg. "You sure are a stubborn one," I grumble, but I can't hide the smile creeping over my face.

"We're two peas in a pod then, Zeke," she says, her lips curling into a mischievous grin. "Perfect for each other." With that, she leans in, her lips brushing against mine, sending sparks through my body.

How does she do that? I was all set to send her away to find a younger man and then she shatters the idea in an instant.

God, I love her.

I *love* her.

She gets up and brushes her hands off on her sweatpants. Then leans down to give me a hand up.

"Wait a sec," I say. I roll up and onto my good leg. It's sore, but at least I didn't bust this one too. "There's something I gotta do. And I want to do it right."

Leaning heavily on one leg, I grab her hand. "I love you, Daisy Barnes...and I never want to be without you, no matter what flies out of my stupid mouth sometimes. Will you make me the luckiest man alive and marry me?"

Daisy blinks, speechless.

Damn, I think I broke her.

"Say somethin', honey," I say, my leg starting to tremble. "I know I don't have a ring, but I'll get you one right away. Any kind you want—oh, wait." I pull a piece of straw out of the egg basket and twist it around her ring finger. "That do for now?"

She swallows slowly then throws herself down next to me, wrapping her arms around my neck. "Yes, oh my god...yes!"

Phew.

Peaches starts yipping happily as Daisy kisses me all over my face, ending on my lips.

"I love you, Zeke Radcliffe," she says, gazing into my eyes. "No matter how much of a pain in my ass you are."

I smile, thinking how blessed I am to have this woman in my life.

Now, if only I could get up without breaking anything else.

EPILOGUE - DAISY

SIX MONTHS LATER

Our wedding reception is going strong well into the night in the old barn. The ceremony was beautiful, intimate, just like I'd wanted, with only our closest friends and family. We can still hear the music and the laughter from the party even as we steal back to the farmhouse, anxious to get away and be alone.

I'm back in Zeke's arms, exactly where I belong, and I smile as he carries me over the threshold—his big, strong, *fully healed* body lifting me as if I were weightless.

Laughing, I wrap my arms around his neck as he kicks the door shut behind us. The roughness of the action matches the intensity of the look in his piercing blue eyes as he gazes down at me, the sultry glare that I've come to know and love focused solely on me, his new bride. My heart flutters to think that I'm the reason for that heated gaze.

"Impatient much?" I tease, running my hands through his thick, dark hair.

He grunts in response, his breath warm on my neck, sending shivers down my spine.

"You should know that well enough by now, woman," he says with a grin.

Without warning, he turns and strides toward the bedroom, his long, purposeful steps making my stomach flip. I giggle again, feeling giddy and excited as he sets me down next to our bed.

"Bend over. Hands on the bed," he demands, and I instantly obey, loving this dominant side of him. In an instant, he's flipped up my wedding dress and pulled down my little white lace panties. He groans and spanks each ass cheek with a firm hand.

"Fuck, that's a beautiful ass," he growls, and I hear him squat down. His lips are kissing me there, and he takes a playful bite.

"Zeke!" I chuckle.

"Spread your legs for me. I wanna make you come before I fuck you from behind."

Oh god... I had already been soaking my panties, but there's a full-blown flood now.

I move my legs apart, still in my heels. He stands and strokes his thick, calloused fingers over my wet folds. I moan as he teases at my clit, while another finger slides into me, slowly moving in and out.

Hell...

He rubs my clit and curls his finger inside me using a steady, deliberate pace, driving the tension in my body higher and higher. I'm writhing and moaning as he works me into a frenzy. Fuck, he knows my body so well.

Suddenly, my legs begin to tremble.

"I'm gonna come, Zeke."

"Yes, come for me, my love." He curls his finger inside me and I detonate.

"Yes! God…oh…*oh!*" I shriek, as he continues his motions and I climax.

Eventually, he slows and takes his hands away. I hear him licking his fingers, then the slide of his zipper. Then I feel his hard cock pressing against my still-throbbing pussy.

He grabs my hips, his hands possessive and urgent as they pull me toward him.

"You're all mine, Daisy," he growls, his voice hoarse as he slides his thick cock into me.

"Yes, all yours," I moan, eagerly shoving my ass back. I want all of him inside me, every inch of this man who has claimed my heart.

He gasps, and in one quick thrust, fills me completely.

His movements are rough yet tender, each powerful stroke a testament to his love for me.

"Zeke…" I whisper breathlessly, urging him on.

He doesn't need any encouragement. His pace quickens, his breath coming in ragged pants, his heavy balls slapping against my skin. I match his rhythm, moving with him, wanting to give as much as I receive. Our bodies move as one, our voices loud.

The tension builds until I'm coming again, screaming his name as my body clenches and convulses.

He screams my name mixed with a series of curses at the ceiling as he finds his release deep inside me, making me pant breathlessly as we come down from the high.

Honestly, there's nothing better than getting plowed by *this* farmer.

As we fall onto the bed in a tangled, sweaty heap, a wave of gratitude for this life and for Zeke washes over me. He's done so much for me: given me a home beyond the big city, taught me how to love such a stubborn and independent man, and shown me how sweet surrender can be, when it's to the right person.

"Welcome home, Daisy Radcliffe," he murmurs, sealing his words with a soft kiss.

~

Now that we've come to the end of the Husky Valley series… what's next?

Frozen Heights

Escape to the enchanting, snow-covered wilderness of Deepwood Mountain's highest peak—*Frozen Heights*—a remote paradise where icy serenity awaits those craving solitude.

Our big, gruff heroes think they're trading in chaos for calm. Little do they know, four strong, spunky women are about to storm into their lives, turning their frosty hearts—*and other parts*—into blazing infernos.

Get ready for plenty of heart-fluttering fun, sizzling chemistry, and enough steam to melt the icicles right off the cozy mountain cabins!

Check out the **Frozen Heights** series page:
https://www.lexihayes.com/series/frozen-heights

You can sign up for my newsletter via my website:
www.lexihayes.com
It's the best way to hear about new and upcoming releases, plus get access to subscriber exclusives and bonus content.

And as always, if you liked this story, please post a review on any of your preferred platforms. Reviews are the lifeblood of independent authors like me, and I welcome your opinions and feedback.

Thanks for reading!

ABOUT THE AUTHOR

Lexi writes short, steamy, over-the-top romance with a heaping dose of humor. She is a long-time superhero lover, book sniffer, and Mr. Darcy fanatic. Raised in the same SoCal city as Will Ferrell, she now resides in sweltering Las Vegas with her husband and two spoiled cats. She dreams of lush green foliage, ocean waves, and Henry Cavill. Or Tom Hiddleston. It's a toss-up really. ;)

Join Lexi's mailing list for new and upcoming releases (and exclusive content!) here: www.lexihayes.com

facebook.com/lexihayesauthor
instagram.com/lexihayesauthor